IDEALITY

By

Kai Alyx Sarus

Grosvenor House
Publishing Limited

This book is published by
Grosvenor House Publishing Ltd
Link House
140 The Broadway, Tolworth, Surrey, KT6 7HT.
www.grosvenorhousepublishing.co.uk

This book is a work of fiction. Any resemblance to
people or events, past or present, is purely coincidental.

A CIP record for this book
is available from the British Library

ISBN 978-1-80381-650-0
eBook ISBN 978-1-80381-651-7

Dedication

Dedicated to Mike.
You will never know your true influence.

To Jasmine,

Thank you for your support on this journey!
I hope you enjoy the ride.

Best Wishes
Kai A. Jaros

13. 11. 23

Preamble

Ideality supposes a distinction between actual reality and the way reality appears to us.

'Happiness is not an ideal of reason but of imagination.'
Immanuel Kant

Dream

Thunder crushed Aurora to the ground. Gasping for air, sweating, her chest palpitating, she woke with a jolt. It was dark in the bedroom as she caught her breath. A bus rolled past her flat, shaking the building, agitating her further.

She turned to look at the clock, familiarity bringing some relief to her wrecked mind. 3.53am. Was it a dream or a nightmare? She felt defeated, deflated, but there was a certain sweetness to the thunder-clap slamming her down so suddenly.

Aurora got up, unsure if she wanted to return to that disturbed sleep. She stumbled in the dark, her arms outstretched to find her way to the bathroom, the darkness comforting. Returning to bed, she relaxed, unable to remember anything of her mental ordeal. Soon she fell into a warm, comfortable sleep.

A dark blue haze obscuring her sight. Standing in a crowded space, bodies she can't see jostling her. Pushing, shoving. The smell of stale sweat arouses her. Miasmatic memories. Lights brightening in front of her, bringing the stage into view. The dark blue haze fazing shifting into electric blue as movement stirs the wispy smoke in front of her. She stands in front of a stage. His voice, enveloping her in surround sound: deep and velvety, like warm aromatherapy oil on skin. The voice from her past, a forgotten life, a buried life. Unable to see him on stage, her memories tugging, dredging, tying her in knots until she feels him, pulling every past feeling and emotion out of her into this time and space. She reaches out to him, just as she had done at those concerts years ago. Arms reaching, desperate to grab a hand, a finger, a splash of sweat.

A lilting melody plays, yanking at her memory. The musical staves like rope entangling her psyche. A lesser-known time. And then the earthquake-inducing crash of drums, electric guitar and bass rip through her. She's jostled as she tries to jump up and down to the rhythmic drums and violating bass. Her favourite band on stage. And then she sees Oliver, as he was when she was 17. Violently jostled, she tries to push back but feels herself overpowered by the crowd she cannot see. She hears herself scream 'Morpheme!' her voice drowned by the music and roaring crowd.

She feels her chest tightening, just as the lights switch from blue to bright white, illuminating the band. Now she is screaming out for help, struggling against the crowd. It wants to hold her back, to control her. The music changes to a softer melody. Oliver walks to the front of the stage, looking directly at Aurora, singing, crooning in a way she can't recall. No, this is different—this isn't their music. She's confused and finding it hard to breathe. Oliver stands tall, dark and grave: short black hair, big blue eyes, angular jaw set in quiet anger. He stops singing and lifts his arms towards her. Come to me. She struggles against the crowd. Someone holds her back. An elbow in the face, a slap in the back of her head, a punch in the ribs. She is encased in a mass of hard angry muscle. Oliver calls her name. Doing so releases her from the horrible weight of angry flesh. She rises into the air, away from the crowd, as if she is floating free from her body. The brightness of the stage hurts her eyes, but she seeks out Oliver, willing herself to him.

He opens his arms wide. Lyrics of a distant song fill her mind. She starts crying as those remembered emotions fill her completely, replacing the last of her will. She is only a metre from him. His arms open to her, singing to her, when she falls hard onto the stage, banging her head and losing consciousness.

Aurora jolted out of sleep again, but this time she remembered the dream: the blue, the warmth of Oliver's voice in contrast to the violence and pain she experienced, and a real fear left her exhausted.

The morning light was penetrating her bedroom. She stared at the ceiling as memories of her teenage years ran riot: music, concerts, friends, fights, anger, Harry, and an impetuous need to claim her existence in a world created by others. And now? She still felt the world was a place created by others, that she had no real choices or power to make it her own. The alarm screamed at her. She slapped it shut and got out of bed.

*

Another cold grey day. Aurora scanned her wardrobe. Tiredness always preferred comfort over form, but she inclined towards her dark purple suit and white blouse to set her mind into work mode. She felt the day stretch out before her like a tarmac runway. Despite the alarm going off, time leaked, minute by minute, and Aurora had to rush to the tube station. The platform was crowded, as Mondays usually were, but there seemed to be an added tension seeping through the tunnel. She fixed her right leg just slightly behind her, as a fail-safe measure, to stop the throng pushing her too close to the edge of the platform. A few men tried to stare her down, intimidating her to move, to shift in their favour. No chance! She was standing her ground.

The stale air, the hot lights and tightly packed crowds increased her body temperature. She felt a line of sweat drawn down her back, the realisation sank in that she would be in an awful state by the time she reached the office. Suddenly, the rumble of the train agitated the crowd and she felt bags and arms in her back. Had she not had her leg locked behind her, she was convinced she would have been pushed into the oncoming train.

Flashes of colour rushed by as the first few carriages passed her. The train stopped and she stood just to the right of one of the doors as she waited for people to leave the train. She was then herded in with people behind her pushing and shoving, only to stop in the middle and not move down. Aurora fought her way through into an aisle and held on. She hadn't even had an opportunity to take out her phone and now she was stuck, unable to let go or move with everyone jammed in.

She stared ahead of her, looking through the other carriages as her mind wandered, escaping the noise and multitudes. What now seemed to be distant memories, shreds of her intense dream, came back to her in sepia and burnt visions.

Why had she dreamt about Oliver? Suddenly, as if some distant life were trying to emerge, the visions seemed very real and intense. Maybe it was just tiredness? Of course, she *was* tired and exhausted. She had spent the last three years of her life struggling through a failing marriage, divorce, and a complete collapse of what she had thought was her emotional life.

Maybe she should take a break with her parents and visit family in Austria and Italy? It had been a long time since she had seen her cousins. David had hated visiting her family, even though he had played the charmer and always made a positive impression. Her anger flared at the thought of him. It was no longer the external heat of the lights and crowds but an internal fire that burned inside her, filtering everything in red and orange. Yes, she needed a break: from him, from work, from everything. To reset and work out what she wanted from life. Her life. The feeling of putting herself first was strange, unfamiliar. Her life had been consumed by David. She was still trying to adjust to being alone, to being a woman approaching her fifties and to being herself.

As a teenager, Aurora had been full of hope and fun. Her parents had been fairly strict but always loving and supportive, allowing her to go out to clubs and concerts with her friends. A small tight-knit group of friends made up her main network and they would always do things together. She wondered what had happened to them. Where were they? What were they doing? Harry?

She hadn't attended any school reunions after marrying David and had fallen out of touch with the group. Toby, Harry, Gretchen and Amber had made up the group with Aurora. They attended most of their classes together and discovered a shared interest in literature and music which tended towards the experimental, preferring to ignore the mainstream. Their teachers loved this as it allowed them to discuss themes and ideas outside of the curriculum, adding depth to the classes.

Aurora had forgotten the impact they had made at college and what an extraordinary experience that had been for the group. And yet, at the time, it had felt like the most natural progression through their friendship, studies and lives. With hindsight, it was easy to see how such an amazing circle of friends could like and support each other in the ways they had.

When Morpheme appeared on the music scene, all five of them connected to the music, but for different reasons. The music and performance brought them even closer together. And then *that* concert. Aurora recalled an activation of intensity in their circle, particularly between Harry and herself. From the depths of her memory, Harry came before her. Wisps of emotion, ghosts of the past flowed and formed in her mind. But then the image was blasted away as the train stopped suddenly and she pushed and pardoned her way off the carriage.

Her dream had made her think about her life. Something she hadn't wanted to do. But it was obvious it was time to take action, time to work out what she wanted from her life.

*

Gretchen, Harry, Aurora, Toby and Amber are queuing outside the Hammersmith Apollo. Excitement energises them and the crowd of fans. Only a handful of police watch from a distance, but so far, so good. This crowd of metalheads is easy compared to the hormone-driven teenage girls who frequent the boyband concerts.

Harry and Aurora are so excited they can hardly speak. They are like one nervous entity. Their expectations of what the next few hours will be are high.

Aurora notices Harry is over-excited, more so than he should be. He can't stand still and seems to be flaring up with heat rash and then shivering. Aurora is disappointed. Harry's reactions mean only one thing and it saddens her. She passes Harry her water bottle, urging him to drink. He pushes it away gently, smiling wide-eyed at her.

Toby and Gretchen exchange looks. Aurora sees this. She is very protective of Harry and immediately hugs him, whispering in his ear. He takes a drink of water. Harry feels her calmness. Suddenly, the energy of the crowd changes. The venue doors open, consuming the mass of humans.

The group is distinct and its members are described as follows:

Toby has shoulder-length dark brown hair, which he keeps immaculately conditioned and styled. As a metalhead, he sets a certain standard in appearance. His clothes, dark but smart and nicely cut, give him an air of a manga hero. All the girls love him and even the boys find themselves drawn to him. He is attractive with big brown almond-shaped eyes, a small nose and curled lips. His skin is pale and unusually free of spots and blemishes. Today he is dressed in black trousers, a ribbed electric blue jumper that contours his developing chest and flat stomach perfectly. Thick-soled blue boots and a long thin black jacket. He looks as if he should be on stage.

Gretchen has deep red hair, which is long and thick, and complements her small pale grey eyes, fine features and porcelain skin. She is wearing her hair tied up and under control in a topknot, giving her an extreme look. She adds to her radical look by wearing a black T-shirt and a long black pencil skirt with a slit on either side. Her knee-high thick black lace-up boots leave only a sliver of her stockings exposed. Gretchen prefers 'black' and 'straight' to any other look and only ever changes her hair and nail colour. Today, her nails are black!

Amber has a quiet confidence about her. She is a modern rock chick, but unlike anything anyone else has seen before. Her individualistic style is determined by her haircut and, luckily for her, her dad owns a salon, so she can exchange work in the salon for incredible and individual hairstyles. Her pecan-brown skin provides the canvas for her vivid and colourful make-up and hair colour palettes. Today, like her name, her naturally curly hair has streaks of amber catching the light, while the sides and back of her head are shaved. Her curls sit on top of her head, afraid to move out of place. Amber's make-up is silvery and pink: contrast and complement. She is wearing a black mesh patchwork crop-top with long sleeves, which she designed and her sister made for her, with straight black trousers. The bright neon thick-soled boots finish off her look. Within the group, they all acknowledge Amber will be the famous one.

Harry and Aurora aren't quite in the same design or style league as their friends. Harry is dressed in a T-shirt with a Morpheme logo, black jeans and burgundy Dr. Martens. He has a short back and sides haircut with a slip of longer hair flopping at the front. It is what makes the girls want to mother him. He is allowed to dye his hair black but strictly forbidden to grow it out long. However, the short style, in intense black, suits his bright blue eyes. People mistake him for the lead singer of Morpheme.

Aurora has long brown hair and she has given it freedom today. It falls in tresses around her, like swaying brown seaweed. She is unsure of make-up so only wears black eyeliner and blue mascara. She is wearing a tight black T-shirt and black jeans. Black and blue trainers stand out against a battalion of boots.

As they surge into the venue, holding out their tickets for inspection, Harry grabs Aurora's hand and the rest of the group form a human chain so as not to lose each other.

They climb up the stairs excitedly and find their places. Amber's father had purchased their tickets all in one go so they could be together. They are at the front of the dress circle and the view couldn't be better.

They are chattering away now that the real excitement has started, re-energised and focused on what the experience will bring. The excitement is like a contagion spreading through the venue. The lights black out and there is a sudden silence in the blackness, like a void that just as quickly is filled with a roar vibrating the space around them like a forcefield. And then the crash of drums and the green lights glare from the stage, creating the illusion of a green dragon entering the space. The feeling is exhilarating. Nothing has prepared the group for this moment as they are transported to a world of sensory overload!

The green lights change to white, like ionised sodium, and the rest of the band appear on stage. No supporting band for Morpheme. They are performing a three-hour set. The venue roars in time to the electrified music. It is no longer filled with individuals, but a collective creature, screaming en masse to its master's beat.

Because that is how it feels to everyone here. They are at the mercy of Morpheme's music. And it is Oliver who controls the music with his presence, his voice, his very being. To every single fan he is the only deity in their pantheon of music. They are his chosen ones. And how good it feels to know you are special, unique, the *only* one.

Each member of the group hardly acknowledges each other as they are lost in their own connections with Oliver and the culture of the stage. They believe in every look sent in their direction, in every smile, and that every word is meant for them. Morpheme invites them into their world, lifting the veil, showing the *real* band; and like love-struck teenagers, the audience falls in love.

Oliver brings audience members up onto the stage. Terrified and in awe, like willing sacrifices, the fans are in shock. Unable to speak, unable to reason, they obey and engage. The rest of the audience thinks they will do better and impress their deity. Those on stage are bewildered sacrifices. And there are no prisoners.

Aurora is enraptured by Oliver. She is so focused on him on stage, she notices nothing of her friends. It is just her and Oliver. His black hair, sharp blue eyes and sultry but powerful voice envelope her. As he starts to sing again, his voice angry and passionate, something inside Aurora ruptures, changing her forever. She feels like a volcano, rent apart to reveal the burning lava flow of her passion. This particular song hits its target. With angry, hard and raw emotion, Oliver's voice rips through the music in contrast to the lovelorn lyrics. The feeling is overwhelming. Tears flow from Aurora's eyes. Nothing can stop the torrent now that it has started. Everything she has felt over the last few years, the stress of Harry's situation, the news, the shit in the world, even her school work and sexual awakening, are all waiting to fall from her. Oliver extracts, pulls and excises the pain, which is why the fans love his performance so much.

Suddenly, she feels Harry's hand in hers and she squeezes it. She cannot face him just now in this vulnerable position because she is always the one in control, the one with the answers, the one Harry can rely on. She feels her weakness and even Harry's tactile support is not enough. This evening she will walk out of the venue a completely different person. She feels this. She feels her life will be different from now on.

Harry is lost in the music until he notices the shimmering and glistening around Aurora's face. She is breathing heavily, unable to catch her breath. Harry watches Aurora without turning directly to her. He knows she is vulnerable now. He knows the emotions coming to the fore. He has experienced this raw pain many times before. Aurora is always there to pick up the pieces. But now she understands him and herself. In a role reversal, Harry is calm and Aurora is the sufferer. It makes Harry think about how he has reached this point in his life. He is grateful for Aurora. Out of their group, she is the one he calls when he is in trouble. She is the one who looks out for him. She thinks she is being subtle, but her inexperience shows in her questions. But that doesn't matter. What matters to Harry is that there is someone in this wide world who looks out for him.

As the song comes to an end, Harry looks at Aurora. She has never looked so beautiful as she does at this moment. The tears shimmer like glitter over her face and evoke images of *Lady Lilith* by Dante Gabriel Rossetti. Harry realises he is lucky to have Aurora in his life. But how will he cope if she isn't there? One day, one day soon, they will live different lives, experience different worlds. And he feels the building swallow him up. He disappears down into the depths of his blackness, deeper than he has ever gone, even deeper than when his father had beaten him and his mother to the point that they were hospitalised.

Harry is numb. He is still holding Aurora's hand. She squeezes his hand, then let's go. Harry feels the last of his resolve shatter into a million shards, only to feel each shard cut him down.

Aurora uses the last of her tissues to clean her face. What is happening to her? How could Morpheme have such an effect on her? She looks at her tissue, noticing a darkness. Her nose is bleeding and she has nothing else to stem the flow. She turns to Harry, who looks pale, even in the obscure light from the stage, and when he turns to look at her now, his reaction is that of someone who has seen death. Aurora shouts at him, but Harry is lost. Amber sees what is happening and passes Aurora a pack of tissues and shouts to her. Aurora nods and they push past to go to the toilets.

It is the interval when Aurora and Amber return to their friends. Harry is sitting down, ignoring Gretchen and Toby, who sign to Amber and Aurora to do something. They all know it can only be Aurora and, as always, she whispers to Harry and they leave their seats.

Aurora speaks to security, saying she needs some fresh air as she has just had a nosebleed. A security person checks their tickets and allows them outside for ten minutes. Even in the waning flame-orange evening light, Harry stands out, white as alabaster.

Pressing a wad of tissues against her nose as red continues to trickle, Aurora asks Harry why he is so quiet. He smiles, in spite of himself. To her questions, he explains he is moved by Morpheme's performance, just as she is. Aurora blushes and her blood gushes. She takes a new tissue. 'That's not fair,' she says, but she cannot help herself and smiles a wry smile. Like close siblings, they know each other well enough to coax the real joy they bring each other. While Aurora is applying another tissue, Harry envelopes her in his arms and holds her, close enough to warm her with his body heat but with enough space to allow her to breathe and move. It is the most emotional contact Aurora will ever experience in her life. She wants to stay here with Harry forever, basking in the now purple glow. She feels centred and happy in this perfect moment.

Harry realises he loves Aurora. His love is for eternity and beyond. He cannot vocalise what he feels for her at this moment or how he has felt about her in the past. Their lives are forever linked through this music. Morpheme is their band and *that* song their anthem.

The security guard calls them over; the interval is almost over. Is she still bleeding? No, the bleeding seems to have stopped: Harry's magical touch. Aurora throws away the blood-soaked tissues. She still has two clean tissues left, just in case. Harry smiles at Aurora. A warm smile, as if he has thawed through her touch. A little redness comes back into his cheeks. A transfusion.

The security guards seem pleased Aurora has stopped bleeding. Having watched the scene between Harry and Aurora, they feel as if they have witnessed something special between two people. They feel privileged. It isn't something they are used to at work.

Aurora and Harry go back to their seats and the group are one again. Aurora gets the kudos for Harry's change, as usual. Only Amber notices the real change in Harry and it worries her.

Morpheme crash back on stage.

Day

Despite Aurora's difficult night, she carried out her morning meetings and tasks with assurance and a smile but felt she needed a little compensation to get her through the day. What that would be she wasn't sure, then Jennie popped her head round the door of Aurora's office.

'Are you free for lunch?'

'Definitely. Is half one OK? I have a meeting at twelve.'

'Perfect. I'll meet you in the lobby then.'

Jennie and Aurora took a short walk round the corner of their building and down a short side street to the local café. It was tucked away, so they were sure to have some privacy. Perfect for a catch-up.

The café had seating for about 30 people. There was dark wood furniture, green-and-white checked tablecloths, landscape artwork on the walls and a large silver and glass refrigerated counter containing an assortment of ingredients. The atmosphere was always warm and friendly and when Tony and Aria got to know you (they knew all their customers), they would happily create any dish for you.

'Where have you been?' asked Aria when Aurora and Jennie walked in. She walked round the counter and came up to Aurora and took her hand.

Turning to Tony, who was busy cooking meatballs, she said, 'Aurora finally comes to visit us.'

Tony looked back, waved, smiled and then returned to the meatballs.

'Come,' said Aria, 'sit here, the best table. I know you like the window seat.'

'Thank you, Aria. What can I say? It's been busy at work. I don't know where the time goes.'

'But you have to eat!' Aria always used this line with Aurora and then proceeded to wheedle out of her where and what she had been eating. Jennie laughed. 'What can I get you to drink?' she asked.

Aurora was feeling guilty about not coming to the café more frequently, so she ordered some water and a smoothie. It might help get her through the afternoon.

Jennie ordered water. They scanned the menu.

'Why don't *you* get the guilty treatment when we come here for lunch?' asked Aurora.

'That's my secret,' laughed Jennie.

'No, you have to tell me. Whenever I come here, I get the third degree. I mean it's lovely to get the attention, but I always feel I'm being told off.'

Jennie laughed and added, 'I order lunch from here at least once a week. Aria always asks about you. I think she has a soft spot for you.'

'Ah, I see. I don't think I'm going to change my habits. I don't like eating out all the time. Don't say anything to Aria though.'

'I won't. Anyway, did you hear about Derek?' Jennie asked, leaning in towards Aurora.

'No, what's happened?'

'Derek's on garden leave,' said Jennie, framing her fingers into inverted commas.

Aria returned with the drinks and waited to take their order. Jennie ordered a cheese omelette with salad, while Aurora ordered the spaghetti vongole, with Aria's approval, who left their table reconciled.

Jennie leaned into the table and whispered.

'There's going to be an investigation... You know what that means, don't you?' She swallowed some water, preparing to go into more detail.

Aurora shook her head.

'So? What has that to do with Derek?' she asked.

'The official line is he's on leave owing to a family crisis, but I saw security with him while he was clearing his stuff out of his desk last night. IT came and confiscated his computer and laptop before he left,' Jennie stated dramatically.

'Do you know who's leading the investigation?' asked Aurora. She wasn't that interested, but she knew Jennie liked to be the in-person with all the knowledge about the company.

'It's an external investigation this time. Probably the FCA and even HMRC too. This one is going to be painful. They'll want to make an example of us.'

'We'll be OK. I mean, how much damage could Derek have done? There are so many checks in place now.'

'Don't be so naïve, Aurora. This is going to be huge, you watch,' said Jennie with a stern look on her face.

Aria brought their order, placing the plates in front of them with a smile. Tony was calling her back.

'Enjoy your meal,' she said, rushing back to the counter.

Aurora tucked into her vongole, suddenly feeling very hungry and glad she had ordered pasta. Aurora wanted to change the subject. She didn't like discussing work at lunchtime and even less when it involved something so serious.

'How's Mike?' she asked Jennie.

Jennie had just taken a mouthful of food. She leaned back in her chair, placed her cutlery down on the plate and finished chewing while holding the napkin to her mouth. She would have tried to answer, only the food was hot.

Aurora smiled and ate another mouthful of pasta.

'Did I tell you about this sudden flurry of calls he's been getting?' Jennie asked as soon as she'd finished chewing.

She had, but Aurora replied, 'I don't think so.'

'I'm sure he's having an affair. Literally, the last month he's been getting call after call in the evenings. The thing is, when he takes the calls, he walks into the bedroom and sometimes they last for 20 minutes.'

'Have you said anything to him about it?'

'Damn right I've said something. He says it's just work because he has a new team and they have a lot of questions. Like I'm supposed to believe that!'

'Does he go out after the calls?' asked Aurora, finishing the last spoonful of spaghetti.

'No, but his work days are longer. He starts earlier and comes home later.'

'Listen, Jennie, Mike is a great guy and he loves you. Trust him. Did you ever think he might be doing some overtime to bring in more money?' Aurora knew Mike wanted to take Jennie away for a romantic anniversary holiday.

'Why do you always take his side?' she asked suspiciously.

'I'm just saying give him the benefit of the doubt. Don't say or do anything for another few weeks and I'm sure everything will work out.'

'We're supposed to be going away on holiday then, but I'm not sure if I want to go with him after this.' Jennie looked down at her half-eaten omelette. It had looked so good to eat when Aria brought it over: hot, appetising, and full of anticipatory promise, but now half-consumed and lukewarm, it was a let-down.

'Don't cancel the holiday. Maybe that's what you both need: to get away from work and have some fun.' Aurora hoped she had got through to Jennie.

'You're right,' replied Jennie. 'I know you are. It's just sometimes I feel life has been a big let-down. When you're young, all you want to do is go out, fall in love, have enough money to have fun. So, you get a job, get married. Then everything changes. It's not enough anymore.'

Jennie looked out of the window. She pushed her plate away.

'You'll be fine. Just don't blow it with Mike. Give him some time and talk to him on your holiday.' Aurora smiled. Disaster averted. She hoped.

Aria returned to clear the plates away. Jennie ordered a cappuccino and Aurora a black tea.

'Have you heard from David recently?' asked Jennie.

'No, thankfully. He's still not paid the money. I wish he would just pay up and then I can be done with it. I just want to forget the divorce, the marriage, every part of that life and move on,' Aurora replied.

'Why do you think he's delaying the payment? I thought the court had awarded you, what... two years ago now?'

'Exactly. He's in contempt of court. I know exactly why he's delaying payment. It's so he can keep some control over me. I can't believe it took me so long to leave him,' said Aurora looking down.

'Don't be so hard on yourself. You've done it now, that's the important thing. Is there anything you can do to make him pay?'

'My solicitor has already done it, but I have to wait while it all goes through the motions. Just as well that I have a good job. Can you imagine if we'd had kids? It doesn't bear thinking about.'

Aria brought the drinks over silently.

'At least something *is* being done.'

Aurora lifted her mug of tea. The mug was hot. The heat felt good in her hands. Why was it whenever David was mentioned, she felt a deep grey coldness, like rain-soaked clothes, penetrate her body?

'What have you got on this afternoon?' Aurora asked Jennie.

'One team meeting and then I'm planning on surprising Alan with a visit to find out what's going on with the investigation.'

'Do you think that's wise? You don't want to put *yourself* in the firing line!'

'You know what it's like, they keep everything quiet. I know the investigation needs to be done, but this is external. They'll want to speak to as many people as possible and this investigation will affect everyone. They shouldn't be allowed to sweep this under the carpet when jobs could be at risk.'

'Do you really think it will come to that?' asked Aurora.

'It's happened before, but they have always managed to disguise it as some restructure or change project. No. We all need to know about this one!' declared Jennie.

They finished their drinks and paid.

'Don't you leave it so long again,' cried Aria as she squeezed Aurora's hand before she left.

They returned to the office—Jennie to her meeting and Aurora to her data analysis. She found herself with a meeting-free afternoon, so she blocked out her calendar to keep it free.

Aurora loved these productive work slots where she was left to concentrate and actually finish a project.

She looked at the clock. 4.30pm. She was tired; her day had been long and busy. She messaged Kerry, her team leader, to say she was leaving for the day and to let the team know. She shut down her computer.

She took a deep breath as soon as she was outside the building. The sky was pale grey, the air damp, and moisture was sticking to her skin. As she left the concourse to walk to the station, large water droplets splashed her head and the pavement. Damn! She had left her umbrella at home. She walked quickly. Would she reach the station before the sky deluged the street? In some vain attempt to avoid the spatter that was increasing in density and repetition, Aurora made herself smaller, scrunching down into some kind of shifting monster. Then a clap of thunder shook the pavement underneath her feet. Only another five minutes and she would be inside the station. But the sky had other plans and while she rushed towards the station, the real rain came tumbling out of the sky. The rain was everywhere: in front of her, behind her, beside her, as if some malevolent being were trying to drown her. In less than a minute, her jacket was soaked. Her purple trousers had turned two-tone from the bottom up and water was sloshing in her shoes. Finally, she reached the tube station, dripping, cold and weighed down under her bloated clothes.

She was exhausted by the time she got home. She stripped and took a shower. The hot water and warmth of the bathroom eased and relaxed her muscles. She thought about Jennie and Mike—and about David. No, she didn't want to think about David. Bloody hell, even after divorce he was still demanding her energy.

Her thoughts turned to the remnants of her dream. How long had it been since she'd listened to those CDs?

She had been a completely different person then: young, ambitious, excited about life, enjoying life. What did she enjoy now? Was the highlight of her week having lunch in a café where she got a bit of motherly attention? Was it finishing a monthly report? Shit! What had happened to her? When had it changed? What was the date, the time, the place, the person, the space? She needed to know!

She racked her brain for a moment but couldn't tie it down to here or there: 30 years ago or 10 years ago. Was it a birthday, holiday, interview, relationship? What was the answer? She thought, *If I knew, could I change it*? *Not in the past maybe, but I would know what to look for in the future. Hmmm… What future?* The only fast thing she had in her life was the rapidly approaching five-zero. Suddenly, that lilting tune came into her mind, the lyrics sung with powerful emotion, and then she recalled the music video and oh, how sweet it was to experience the full sensual emotion of that performance. It overwhelmed her, just as it had done countless times before, this particular song, punching her in the stomach and ripping out all her insides, making her cry with the pain of a shattered heart. She sobbed, her chest and shoulders heaving. The whole emotional mess poured out, beating in time to the song until she was left just a standing facade, dripping from the internal rain.

Then life interrupted. She realised what this meant. It was the everyday minutiae of life, the outside world clambering for her attention, distracting her, pulling her away from that inner world of delicious power. She nabbed the opportunity, ran into the bedroom still wet and naked and wrote it down. Date. Time. Place. Space. In attendance. There, she had trapped the moment.

Incredible as it was, this realisation gave Aurora the power to control her life. When she had been married, and even when she had lived at home with her parents, there were constant interruptions to her life's passions.

She didn't begrudge her parents this time; they had always had her best interests at heart and supported everything she wanted to do. But they didn't understand it. And that meant they wouldn't think twice about booking a family get-together when Aurora had an important exam to revise for, assuming she was always available for their activities. They never once asked her if she had anything else on.

David was different. He knew exactly what he was doing and why he was doing it. He clearly felt he had a right to sabotage any of her hobbies and passions. But he would always make sure her work and work-related exams were protected. He benefitted too much from that to risk interfering that far. Aurora hadn't noticed the patterns or changes in behaviour until years later when she realised David's behaviour towards her relied on money and control. Considering she was the one bringing in the money, she was completely shocked when a psychotherapist friend had stated this scenario rather bluntly at dinner. That had been one of those epiphany moments for Aurora. The fogginess in which her marriage was fading suddenly disappeared and the reality of her experiences shocked and angered her.

However, extricating herself from David was harder than she thought possible. So many connections, links, ties and psychological pulls she had not expected. The first split from David was a relief, but she missed something. There was a gaping wound that made her feel exposed and vulnerable and despite David being the one who had slashed open that wound, Aurora felt he was the only one who could heal it. How wrong had she been?

After six months away from him, Aurora felt the pull too keenly to ignore it. What she should have done was stick it out, get over the worst of the shock to her system, but she gave in. She took the easy way, the less painful way, hoping David, in his changed manner, would heal her. After all, he said he loved her...

It didn't take long for him to revert to his controlling behaviours. But they were so subtle, Aurora didn't really notice. Those little things that seem so insignificant, petty, trivial and immaterial that you constantly brush them away like breadcrumbs, chastising yourself for being so low! But those insignificant, petty, trivial and immaterial things are the indicators, the red flashing light, the fire alarm, the siren, the distress signal, warning you.

Aurora felt her instinct had abandoned her, or had she abandoned it? Unable to trust herself, she no longer looked inside herself to question, query, and solve emotional tasks. Slowly, creeping, crawling, David disarmed Aurora's instinct until she relied only on his way of thinking. She gave herself completely and lost her essence. She was no longer a separate entity, a woman, an individual, but became subsumed into his being, his existence.

And then the accident happened. David was in hospital. It was critical. His body crushed by the impact of the SUV. His much-loved GSX Hayabusa irreparable: dead. The doctors said there was hope for David to pull through, although full recovery might take years. There was no hope for the bike. David cried when told. It was the only time Aurora had seen him really cry. Not even when he was told by the doctors he might not be able to ride again did he cry. Not for himself, not for Aurora, who was emotionally wrecked seeing him in that crushed state, but for the dead bike. Aurora put it down to trauma.

There is always an emotional excuse we can conjure up to mitigate behaviours; we just need to find the right one to fit the circumstance. And it was easy for both David and Aurora to push all their relationship incapabilities and betrayals into the TRAUMA box. It suited them both that they didn't have to talk about uncomfortable, evil truths that sat there like black leeches gorging on hypocrisy and denial.

After a month in hospital, David was released in a wheelchair. Oh, how the nurses and hospital staff would miss him: a perfect patient and such a lovely smile!

How did he do that, even in such a state? There were outpatient visits of course: physiotherapy, psychotherapy, blood tests, eye tests, another CT scan, just to make sure. And Aurora was there for every appointment.

Suddenly, with David at home, only a single but still decent salary coming in, and Aurora having just started a new job in an accountancy firm, Aurora seemed to be in charge. While Aurora worked, cared for David, and ran the household, running on adrenaline, David had time on his hands and on his mind. He spoke to Aurora in any way he wanted. It was not the voice of the much-loved hospital patient; it was the voice of a man who had wobbled on his pedestal and realised his precariousness. It was a man fighting for control over his life and that of his wife.

Even though Aurora could have lost David in the accident, David felt he could have lost Aurora. Lying in the hospital bed, conscious but silent, David made himself a double victim: the loss of his bike and potentially his wife. But the thought process of someone who has no other task ahead of them than to make their body live is erratic and overwhelming. When do we get the opportunity simply to think? When in our lives does the opportunity arise that we no longer have to consider or expend energy on eating, sleeping, working, shitting. When that is all done for us, there is nothing else to do but think. And David thought.

Aurora thought she noticed frowns, eyelids flickering, and the mouth tightening while sitting watching David by his hospital bed. Her instinct screamed at her that David was conscious and was thinking about his situation. She whispered his name. The eyes stayed closed and the reactions stopped. Her instinct, limited as it was, shut down and she let her inner screaming fade into the TRAUMA box.

Had Aurora seen David's thoughts bounding through his psyche, she would have really screamed and left him there and then.

She continued to deny her instinct. She deprived it of power, guillotined any resurrection until her only emotional input came from David.

And now? She was far from his influence, but she had to find herself again. Find that instinct *inside* herself. Her *essence*. She returned to the outer world.

*

She picked up her post and looked through the white envelopes: bill reminders, demands for payment. They had reverted to the real, handheld notices, going beyond the electronic. She opened them all, put the letters to one side and the envelopes in the recycling bin. She put a pizza in the oven, opened her laptop and set to destroying the horrible bills.

Checking her bank account, she was shocked to find her bank account in credit by over £300,000. The payee was David. He had finally made the payment promised more than a year ago and decided by the courts two years before. Never again would she have to speak to him. It was all the money! The realisation that she finally had some control over her life was bittersweet. She had waited so long for her twisted life to right itself, but now that it was happening, she was unsure of herself, of what she wanted to do, if anything. But at least having her money back was a start.

That evening she ate her dinner in silence. No television, no music, just listening to the thrash of the rain against her windows.

Disaster

Three weeks after Jennie's lunchtime premonition, Aurora was in the office kitchen making a cup of tea when she heard a couple of colleagues whispering just by the door.

'Another financial train wreck caused by aggressive management tactics. As long as the money's coming in for shareholders and the directors, they don't care what happens to staff.'

'You can't blame shareholders; they were just as blind to what was going on as we were.'

'If you think that, you are just as stupid and blind as the rest of them. It's too convenient for them when people like you say that. They know exactly what is going on. Don't think for one moment that if there was a choice between CSR and making another pound on their returns, they wouldn't go for the money. I attended those shareholder meetings. As long as they were getting those quick returns, they allowed the directors to do anything they wanted. You know, in the five years I've attended those meetings, not one management proposal was rejected.'

'But that's why shareholders invest: to get a return.'

'Yeah, to get a return, with blood on their hands while they hold them up in defence and say "I didn't know." They supported the structural change that gave Derek and Richard control over the pension scheme, to "speed things up, reduce bureaucracy, create higher returns and quicker financial turnarounds". God, what a mess!'

'You'll be alright though; you refused to pay into the company pension. At least you've still got your money.'

'But how can I be pleased with that after the way I was treated? Two promotion opportunities lost, subtle threat of a shit reference if I left, my team made redundant, ha, that's a joke. They might as well have been fired for any redundancy payment they'll receive. There is no win here as far as I'm concerned.'

'Look, we'd better go; they're calling teams into meetings. Call me later.'

'This won't be the end of it.'

Aurora was shocked. The full force of what was happening around her had not penetrated her consciousness. She was always behind, catching up, trying to see what others saw, but too late. What would she do if she were made redundant? No, that wouldn't happen. They needed to keep her team. Half the company staff had already been let go, and she and her team were still there. It wouldn't come to that, she was sure.

Aurora should have paid more attention to Jennie's concerns and interest in the investigation. The investigation into financial irregularities had thrown up full fraud and embezzlement charges. The company pension had been raided and left with a 'nominal balance'. This was more than just mishandling funds. The company was no longer a going concern. Redundancies were made, assets broken up and sold. Staff who had paid into the NSM company pension lost all their savings. The full horror of what had happened was only made clear when the figures were released. NSM had not invested any contributions for their staff; they had just taken staff contributions and used them for high-risk investments to get better returns for the key directors. A full investigation would now be conducted, but it was too late for the company and its employees. Aurora recalled how aggressive the company had been in promoting their own pension fund and virtually blackmailing staff into signing up with them. Staff were actively discouraged from seeking independent financial advice and paying into an external pension.

Aurora returned to her office when Jacqui appeared.

'Where have you been? We're being called into a meeting with HR,' she said, gesturing to Aurora to follow her. Aurora felt light-headed as she got up again and hurried to the main meeting room where the rest of her team were already seated.

The HR director, operations director and a senior auditor from the investigating team were there to oversee the administration process. Rebecca Grant, the HR director, spoke to the team. She explained that due to the outcomes of the investigation, the company was going into administration and unfortunately this meant they had to let staff go. Further to the fact that there was no money, regrettably, they could only pay one month's salary as a redundancy offer to everyone.

She said that all employees would receive the current month's salary in addition to that and that the FCA were looking into compensation for staff in line with any money invested with the company. She then advised them all that they would have to collect their personal belongings and leave the building. Wage slips and P45s would be emailed. Finally, she thanked them all for their service.

Aurora blinked. She looked at Rebecca. What was she saying?

Jacqui started crying. Graeme started swearing before walking out of the meeting room. The others just looked at Aurora for some kind of answer but could see she was just as shocked as they were.

That was it: 'Here is your P45 and there's the door.' Seven years of hard work and loyalty and this is what she had to show for it. Less than £8,000 after taxes. She felt numb and unsure of herself, but she still had a duty to her team, so she spoke to each of them while they were being watched by security.

'Fucking arseholes. How can they sleep at night?'

'Graeme, please calm down. I know you're angry, we all are, but this is not helping.'

'Maybe not, but it makes me feel better. What are they going to do? Have me arrested for swearing? Fire me? Been there, doing that!'

'Graeme, please, think about your family.'

'That's what makes me angry. I do think about my family. It's why I stayed at this fucking company for so long.

The pension was supposed to be great. I could invest in my kids when they're older, pay off my mortgage, have a comfortable retirement. Now all that is gone and not just gone, but it was a lie from the start.'

There wasn't much Aurora could say to make things better. Graeme was right; whole lives were irreparably wrecked by this disaster.

'Graeme, look at me,' said Aurora. 'You need to focus on getting another job and take some time with your family. This is not your fault. You haven't done anything wrong, but you need to take steps. Graeme, are you listening to me?'

He looked up at Aurora. His eyes were red and glistening. He closed his bag and shook Aurora's hand.

'I'm going home. Don't worry, I won't let you down. I'll be in touch.'

Aurora watched him leave, escorted by the building security.

'I know my way out. You don't have to treat me like a fucking criminal,' he shouted at the security guard who looked around the office nervously.

Aurora rushed over and asked the guard to stay and permit Graeme to leave alone.

'But I'm supposed to escort people off the premises.'

'He will leave the building. Don't worry. There are others still here. Come with me, I need to get my things,' said Aurora, coaxing the guard to follow her and forget Graeme.

She packed the few personal items she had in her drawer, shut down her computer and left her keys and pass on the desk. She wouldn't need them anymore. She left her office and walked past her team's section. After Graeme's outburst, she was worried the others might be even more upset. Kerry and the others had been swiftly escorted out of the building. Only Jacqui was still sitting at her desk crying, seemingly unable to move. The other guard appeared as Aurora and her guard reached Jacqui's desk.

'Jacqui? Let's get your things and go for a drink,' whispered Aurora, trying to manoeuvre her into action.

Jacqui looked up at Aurora and smiled with recognition. She looked around her, found her bag and put her few belongings away. She opened her drawers, which were already emptied of any paperwork. There was nothing else she had to take. She seemed bewildered and confused by events. She stood up, put on her jacket and started in the direction of the lift.

'Miss, I need your pass and any keys you have,' said the security guard.

'Oh, sorry,' she replied, frowning. She took the items from her jacket pocket and placed them on her desk.

Aurora looked at both guards.

'I'll make sure she's OK. I'll take her in the lift. You don't need to follow us.'

One of the guards made a move to follow them when Aurora turned to him.

'I said we are leaving. You can check the damned security cameras to make sure. Do you understand!' The guard stopped where he was, halted by Aurora's look and tone.

Once they were in the lift, Jacqui started to sob. Aurora took her to a small café. She bought Jacqui a hot chocolate and herself a Darjeeling tea. Just before she paid, she ordered two slices of marble cake. Jacqui had found a quiet corner at the back of the café and was sobbing into her third tissue.

'Thank you.'

'You're welcome, Jacqui.'

They sat quietly for a moment while the drinks cooled. Aurora started eating her cake, but Jacqui continued to stare out into the café, past Aurora.

Jacqui took a sip of her drink and held onto the hot mug. A visible shiver ran through her.

'It's OK for you,' she started, still staring out into the distance.

'You're still young enough to start again. I'm 57 years old. I was expecting to retire in five years with a nice healthy pension. What am I going to do now?'

Her face was pale and she looked worn from crying. Aurora saw Jacqui for the first time, a vulnerable woman who felt she had lost everything.

'Don't you have other pensions from your previous jobs?' asked Aurora, trying to find some kind of positive take.

'Huh. I believed them. I believed everything they told me. They have taken more than my money. They assured and persuaded me my money was safe, my returns would be guaranteed. I believed them completely. I trusted them when they convinced me to move my other pension funds into the NSM pension. I believed them when they said they would grant 12 per cent bonus on any other funds transferred into the company pension. I put everything I had in there!' she said, looking at Aurora. 'I have nothing,' she whispered, crying into her hot chocolate. She put the mug down and took out a new tissue.

Aurora was stunned. She recalled the conversation she had heard outside the kitchen. Why hadn't Jacqui sought independent advice? Aurora had considered the same pension offer, but when she'd discussed the terms with her advisor, she'd dissuaded her from going ahead with any transfer, advising it would be better to keep her current pensions where they were. Aurora recalled a number of colleagues she had told about her advisor's suggestion, who had scoffed and laughed at her for being so risk-averse. You could never make any money if you didn't take risks! Now she felt like showering her advisor with flowers!

But what could she do about Jacqui? What options were available to a woman in her position? No FCA compensation package would be able to cover all of her losses.

'Jacqui, I know you don't want to hear this now, but why don't you contact a legal firm to see if there is anything they can do? I can put you in touch with my financial advisor as well—there is no charge for her advice.' Aurora hoped this would give Jacqui something to think about.

Jacqui changed her focus and looked at Aurora.

'What did you say?'

'I suggested speaking to a legal firm and an independent financial advisor.'

'Yes. OK. Good idea,' she replied distantly.

Aurora finished her cake and tea. Jacqui had hardly touched hers.

'I want to go home now,' she said standing up.

'I'll come with you,' said Aurora, slightly concerned by the sudden change in Jacqui.

'Why?'

'I just want to make sure you get home OK. Today has been a big shock for all of us.'

'No need. I'll be fine.'

They left the café. Jacqui turned to Aurora and hugged her—tight.

'Thank you,' she whispered in Aurora's ear and then walked towards the tube station.

Aurora watched Jacqui for a few seconds, wondering if she would see her again. The thought sent a shiver down her spine and she vowed she would call her the next day.

*

Returning home Aurora was emotionally drained. Having tried to support her team and done what she could, she was now left to consider her own situation. She wrapped herself in a navy blue blanket and lay down on the sofa. Had she at least had a decent redundancy package, that would have helped her feel more in control, have some power over her circumstances, but she had had no time to think or plan her future. Even with the money she had, it wasn't enough for a comfortable retirement and, although she still had her other pensions, she had lost seven years of savings at NSM. The conversation with Jacqui dawned on her. She herself was approaching 50. How would she be viewed in an interview? As an interviewer, she had been prejudiced towards those showing more energy and enthusiasm for roles. She had been guilty of believing the hype people presented of themselves, promising victories, providing their own testimonials of their dazzling achievements, only for it to have all been bravado and bullshit. How many 'incredible' people had they hired only for them to be lazy, rude and self-motivated.

Aurora's mind raced through the day's events. She found it hard to settle down. Flashes of the meeting room appeared in various shades of blue, reflecting her mood. She shivered and wrapped the blue blanket round her tighter, tucking in the edges to encase herself. Her mind darted in numerous directions, none of which was pleasant. She felt uncomfortable and anxious. Her muscles contracted, her heart and chest crushed in as if a wrecking ball was swinging for her every second while she was frozen, unable to move away from the strikes. Her body compressed until she got smaller and smaller. Suddenly, the blanket was suffocating her and she kicked it off. She couldn't breathe. She got up to open a window, but the strain of the day, of the last few weeks was released; the reality of Aurora's situation tormented her mind so completely that she felt nauseous and faint. She lay back down on the sofa and fell into an aggravated unconsciousness.

*

Aurora's back in the meeting room. A pale blue hue encases the space. She is alone as Rebecca Grant enters the room, her skin tinged blue. She speaks to Aurora, but Aurora can't hear her faint voice; only a few words release their meaning. Aurora leans in closer, focusing on Rebecca's mouth, as she is so keen to hear the words. What is Rebecca saying? Aurora understands the words 'mistake' and 'employed', but there is no context. Rebecca continues to speak and animate, but it is no use. Aurora tries to say something, attracting Rebecca's attention so she can ask her to speak up. Rebecca just keeps talking. The blue hue passes into a blue haze, Rebecca's talking fades out into the distance until there isn't even a whisper. Aurora is sinking into a black space. Not a room, not a hole, just a black space. Aurora is walking straight ahead. A green mist appears, growing thicker, arranging itself into images as yet unrecognisable. She doesn't understand what is happening. She wants Rebecca to stay away. She is pulled into thickening green mist until she finds herself looking at a stage. She relaxes. There is a band on stage, and green lights flash. She calls out to Oliver. She needs him now. She needs his passion, his energy. She holds out her arms to him, beckoning him to her. She feels strange strong arms slip around her waist and hold her tight. Oohhh, how good it feels to be held! She turns to look behind her and sees David! She screams and tries to free herself, but he holds on tight, squeezing, gripping. He's smiling and whispering, 'I will save you', but all she wants is to free herself from David and be with Oliver who is still on stage, oblivious to her screams. She feels David crushing her from behind. She can no longer scream. She is crying, begging David to let her go, stress and strain causing her to catch her breath. And then blackness as she screams out and wakes up on the sofa.

Decision

Aurora's nights continued in this vein. Her mind continued to flit between dark colours, antagonising images and a depth of violence that scared her. There was no such thing as a quiet night's sleep anymore. It was all phantoms and visions, as if she were in some Gothic nightmare.

She awoke in a cold sweat. Searching for solace, she looked at the clock. 5.47am. Exhausted, but unwilling to suffer further mental abuses, she got up from her bed and had a shower.

It had been a fortnight since she had been exorcised from NSM. Every day the redundancy became more real to her and the impact of it on her situation starker. Financially, she was secure. The money that David had finally paid was hers anyway, but the timing of its payment was key in her decision to take some time and think about the direction of her life.

Her financial security contrasted with Jacqui's insecurity. Aurora thought about the financial reality for so many people, including her team at NSM. Some of them would be fine; they would go on to achieve career objectives and have enough time to claw back their losses. But those people like Jacqui? My God, how could you claw back anything near those losses? A lifetime of saving in ten years? It just couldn't happen. Aurora called her.

'Hello, Jacqui, it's Aurora. How are you?'

'Oh, Aurora, OK. No, not OK. I can't seem to think or move. My life has fallen apart and I don't know how to fix it. Everything just feels impossible. What am...'

'Jacqui?'

'What am I going to do? I can't even stop crying.'

'I feel like all the fight has gone out of me. I have no strength left to start again. I just want to fade away. No one cares about me anyway. You're the only person from NSM to have called me. You know that? No one else. Not even HR have followed up to make sure I got the paperwork. My friends haven't called or asked how I am. My brother and sister just talk around the redundancy. I can feel they don't want to talk about it; they feel awkward. It feels as if I've died and people are just tiptoeing around me...' cried Jacqui.

Aurora could hear the stress in her voice, the frailty, as if Jacqui had aged overnight. The cracks in her voice illustrating the very real but invisible cracks in her life. But what could she say to Jacqui to support her, make her feel better, make her understand that she wasn't on her own?

'Jacqui, I can't fix what has been done. I can't make any promises to you. But I can be here for you. I know you probably don't want to hear this right now, but you do need to *do* something. Talk to my financial advisor at least. I'll introduce you over email and you can arrange a chat with her. She'll be able to make some sense out of the mess and help you with next steps.'

'What next steps? I don't even have a job. How am I going to get a job at my age? Who would want me when my own family and friends can't even look me in the face? I appreciate your call and your help, but I don't see the point in any of this.'

'What do you mean?'

'The point of my life. Why am I here just trying to exist?'

'Jacqui?'

'No, really Aurora, I can't do it anymore. I just don't want to wake up again...'

'Jacqui?' shouted Aurora as her own voice echoed back to her from the black screen.

As unwell and raw as she felt, Aurora got up, threw some clothes on and rushed over to Jacqui's flat in a taxi.

*

Aurora didn't have a plan for what she would do with Jacqui, but it was clear she had to do something. As she reached her block of flats, she worried about getting in, but just as she reached the main entrance door, someone came out and she rushed in. This was the first time she had been to Jacqui's flat, so she had to find her way around the building. Finally, she reached the door of Jacqui's flat and knocked.

'Who is it?' asked an angry voice. Aurora did not recognise Jacqui's voice. It was deep and trembling with an anger Aurora had never heard from her before.

'Jacqui, it's Aurora. Can you let me in?'

'What are you doing here?'

'I came to see you because I was worried about you. Let's go out and get a drink.'

'No. You shouldn't have come.'

'Jacqui, please. I came all this way. Can I at least have a glass of water?'

Aurora could hear sobbing behind the door. She just needed to get inside, convince Jacqui to open the door. She waited, not wanting to hurry her, but every second stretched out to an invisible horizon like long shadows.

'Jacqui, I really need a drink. Please?'

Aurora couldn't hide the desperation from her voice. Then she heard the door chain scrape across the restrictor. She gasped in anticipation that she might just have reached Jacqui in time. She waited, holding her breath, not wanting to miss any sound that might imply failure.

The door opened ever so slightly. Jacqui's face, puffed and red with crying and emotional stress, appeared in the gap. Aurora smiled and held out her hand. Jacqui looked completely defeated and allowed Aurora inside.

'You should have left me on my own. You shouldn't have come, Aurora.'

'Can I have that glass of water, please?'

Jacqui looked up at Aurora. She was confused but went into the kitchen. She handed the glass of water to Aurora.

'Thank you. I like the decor in your flat: very warm and comfortable. How long have you lived here?'

'Um, thank you. I've lived here for six years now. Look, Aurora, I'm really sorry, but please go.'

'I'm not leaving you on your own, Jacqui. So, your choices are, I can either stay here and we can order in something to eat, or I'm happy to cook, or you pack a few things and come over to my place for a few days.'

'What are you doing?'

'We both know what you were going to do and what I'm doing here now, Jacqui, don't we?'

Jacqui fell down onto the sofa and cried. Only there were no tears left, just a rasping noise, like a pestle and mortar grinding against each other.

Aurora stayed with Jacqui for two nights. She was emotionally exhausted, but relieved. She had got Jacqui through the dark tunnel and out the other end, but it had cost her a little bit of herself and she felt it, like a chipped porcelain statue.

Thinking about it, Aurora hadn't felt as if there was any big dramatic effect, no big drama involving emergency services or hospital admissions. It had been a small act, a phone call, a visit, an understanding of what was at stake for Jacqui. She had put herself in between Jacqui and the blackness. She couldn't say the word as she didn't want to evoke it. But she felt the cold chill of what could have been had she not acted. She realised with a sinking depression that everyone could take that path at some point in their lives. Intervention was the only way to mitigate it. And she hoped that the people in her life would intervene, even if it meant putting themselves in the firing line. She wondered what it took to spot, realise and take action to stop someone journeying to the final destination. In Jacqui's case, it had been her voice that had alerted Aurora to an uncomfortable feeling. Were there other clues?

By the time Aurora returned home, having made sure Jacqui had friends coming over to stay with her and a plan of action regarding her finances, she was physically and mentally exhausted. Releasing herself from the responsibility for another person released the stresses and strains of what she had gone through. Although a different situation, it felt similar to her escape from David. It was beyond relief. It was a psychological shift that placed her in a completely new space.

Taking a deep breath, Aurora felt her core give way and she fell asleep crying. For herself, for Jacqui and for the world.

*

Aurora woke up in the night with a fever and nausea unlike anything she had experienced before, leaving her unable to do anything except crawl between bed and bathroom. She felt awful: shivers, unable to eat, the thought of food causing her to vomit, aching body and a lethargy that turned her body to lead. She could hardly speak and spent three days in bed with water and aspirin. People left messages. Worry set in when there was no reply. Aurora found it too difficult to engage even in messaging. She forced herself to send holding messages and hoped people would leave her alone to sleep. By the end of the third day, she was feeling slightly better and hunger crept back, but she had very little food and no energy to get up to cook.

Aurora called her parents. They were obviously concerned for her health. Wanting to show support and that they were still very able, they insisted on visiting Aurora at home.

Aurora hadn't realised how much she had missed her parents. They arrived to find her still in pyjamas. Bringing food, Aurora's father, Francesco, cooked her favourite childhood meal: pumpkin dumplings with butter and fresh herbs. All her stresses and strains dissipated as her parents cared for her. Aurora fell into a deep and restful sleep while her mother, Anna, read to her. Aurora promised herself she would make more time for her parents.

When Aurora woke from her long nap, she found herself in darkness. As her eyes adjusted to the dark room, she thought her parents' visit must have been a dream. A nice, warm, loving dream. She felt so much better now her fever had broken and some energy had returned to her limbs that it was no longer an effort to get out of bed. And her appetite had returned with gusto. What could she eat? She sat up in bed and drank some water. The cool liquid seeped through her body, bringing further relief after the fiery illness that had gripped her body for several days.

She put on her dressing gown and stepped into the hall, bumping into her mother, who had just come out of the bathroom. Both women scared each other but then laughed in relief and Aurora hugged her mother tightly.

They walked into the lounge and sat down. Francesco was reading *Dine Out* magazine. He looked up and put it aside before standing up to hug Aurora.

'How are you feeling, Aurora?' he asked, his face strained and serious.

'I'm better. I don't feel so tired now. Thank you for being here, both of you,' she said squeezing Anna's hand.

'You'll always be our little girl, Aurora. I know you don't like it when I say that, but it's true. We were so frightened when we spoke to you the other day. So many things have gone wrong. But look at you now, you look so much better and you're hungry!'

'Well, Aurora, what would you like to eat? Name anything.'

Aurora thought for a moment, smiling. Her parents had always done everything together. They were one and the same person and knew what the other was thinking. What an offer to have her dad cook her anything she wanted! She knew he would be disappointed if she asked for her favourite meal again. Since selling off the restaurant, he missed the hustle and bustle of the hospitality business and took every opportunity to cook for others.

'Baccala' Campagnolo,' stated Aurora.

'Perfect! I'll be back in half an hour,' said Francesco as he stood up from the armchair.

'I'll come with you,' said Aurora.

'No, you won't,' stated Anna firmly. 'You still need to rest. I'll make you a cup of tea while your father goes out shopping.'

'Your mother is right. Rest. I'll be fine, I know where I'm going. I noticed an Italian deli up on the High Street.' Kissing both women on the forehead, he left, humming to himself.

'You know your father likes to cook and he's so happy to be here for you. Come in the kitchen with me,' she said, taking Aurora's hand and seating her at the small bistro table.

Anna made two cups of tea.

'Mum, this is wonderful. What is it?'

'It's that lovely Japanese sencha tea I told you about. I order it from The Tea House. Doesn't it taste so fresh and natural?'

Aurora sipped the hot refreshing tea that tasted of nature. It renewed her energy. Whether it was psychological, social or physiological, she didn't know, but drinking tea from those dried green leaves from another land, where they had been tended and cared for, where Nature had worked her miracle through soil and weather, brought about a feeling of positivity and confidence within herself. She felt OK.

Anna sat down opposite her at the tiny table. She wanted to talk. The kitchen was always the place to discuss, chat, share, figure out, resolve problems and Aurora knew Anna wanted to discuss: her situation.

'Aurora, you know we will always support you in any decisions you make,' said Anna looking at her daughter for acknowledgment. Aurora nodded.

'If you need a break, some time away, why don't you visit Nathalie and Tobias? They are hoping to take some holiday time and were asking if your father and I wanted to visit. I was thinking it might be a nice break for you to go instead. I want you to get better. You need a break after all this stressful business.'

'Thanks, Mum. I really appreciate it. But I think I need to work out what it is I want to do next. I would be happier taking a break if I knew what I was coming back to. I would love to see Nathalie and Tobias again, but I need to sort out my life first!' replied Aurora with a wan smile.

'Are you sure?'

'Yes. Mum, I really appreciate you and Dad being here. I don't say it enough, but I love you,' she said as her mother's face softened into a blur of colour.

Anna stood up and hugged her daughter.

'I love you too, Aurora.'

They sat down again.

'When you're feeling better, do call Nathalie and Tobias. They would love to hear from you and maybe you can organise a visit later in the year.'

'I will,' replied Aurora, wiping her eyes with her pyjama sleeve.

'I'm glad you got the money back at last. Has David called you?'

'No, thankfully. I think he's finally left me alone. At least, I hope.'

'You're still nervous about him, aren't you?'

'It's only because I had a bad dream the other night. It makes me feel uneasy.'

'Why don't you move, or come and stay with us for a while? Or you can stay over while we're away and have some time to yourself.'

'I don't want to keep running away. Besides, I need to work out what I want to do. That might involve travel, so I might not even be here that much.'

'Alright, but do call us if anything happens. Don't leave it for so long again. You need to be safe. He's shown what kind of person he really is, so don't take any risks. I can't bear to think what could happen to you... if he came back.'

'Mum, don't do this to yourself. Please don't cry. Look, I promise I will let you know if anything happens, OK?'

They held hands, tightly. Anna looked at her daughter and wiped Aurora's tears with her hand, stroking her cheek, like she had when Aurora was very young. Aurora nuzzled her face into her mother's hand, still as soft as it was forty years ago.

Francesco walked into the kitchen carrying two bags of shopping. It was time to vacate the kitchen.

*

Aurora faced a period of indecision about her next career move. Should she take the risk and do what she'd always wanted to do? The stress of the unknown, taking her future into her own hands, frightened her. But why? She had proved in her finance career that she could make an impact, create outcomes and make good decisions. Surely, saving millions of pounds in benefits for stakeholders was scarier than taking control over her own life? Aurora stood by the window, thinking about her dilemma, but was it really a dilemma? Wasn't it the fact that if she failed, it would be her fault and no one else's? Full responsibility meant just that. If a new career move didn't work out, she would be a failure. And what did that mean to her? What was the failure that was crippling her decision-making? She couldn't even name it. There wasn't one specific 'failure' that scared her, it was just the big black thing, an obstruction, a monster with changing features, like Zola's Le Voreux, or Miyazaki's No-Face. Always there, always waiting for the mistake that would lead to disaster. Her mind raced with images of jeering crowds and people laughing at her. Wasn't that the frightening part? The derision, the ridicule, the contempt? But where did this horrible feeling come from? At what point did it materialise? She had never felt like this before, never felt incompetent or unable to do things. She had always approached her work and career with enthusiasm and a problem-solving attitude. So why did the idea of attempting something new terrify her into paralysis? How could she defeat that monster? Aurora sighed. What did she always do when faced with a problem at work? She read. She learned. She solved the problem. She recalled the Charlotte Perkins Gilman poem, 'An Obstacle'. That was what she needed to do: just act as if the 'failure' was not there. She needed to focus on the job in hand and not fantasticate the process.

With that in mind, she planned her next move.

Debut

The easy part was buying a new laptop, paper pads, pens and a dictionary. Then she dug out her dissertation and some of her early work that she had done when she first started in insurance marketing to get a sense of what she had achieved. The difficult part was knowing where to start. She was unknown and had to make a name for herself. The easiest way was to start locally. She created a list of local pubs that carried live music nights promoting new music. She also found some small venues that held regular band nights. Aurora set up a blog site and a few social media channels. Why beg for a job when she could post her own articles and market them?

After three weeks of running around local pubs and bars, she was getting some traction on her blog. After her first full month of self-employed work, Aurora celebrated with a takeaway and a night in. She'd received her first fee for some photos and a review to be published in the local newspaper. It wasn't much, but it was a start.

The following week she went to the Dog and Duck pub, only twenty minutes' walk from her flat. She had avoided its run-down look and unfriendly appearance but her contact at the local newspaper told her to try it out.

The pub had recently been lucky enough to be associated with a number of upcoming artists and it was down to the pub manager, who seemed to have a golden touch when it came to showcasing new artists. Aurora knew this was a good tip and she had to go, but she dreaded it.

Arriving at the pub by five o'clock, she found it quiet and only half full: mainly middle-aged men who looked like the fixtures of the pub. They stared at her. *This was a bad idea*, Aurora thought. She went over to the bar and asked to speak to the manager. He was nothing like Aurora expected. He looked as if he'd only just left school. With soft white skin and large brown eyes, he put her in mind of an anime character. She introduced herself and asked if he would mind her staying to review the bands. He was surprised.

'Not at all. Thanks for the notice. Most people just turn up and demand free drinks,' he replied smiling. 'My name's Nigel.' And he held out his hand.

'Aurora.'

And they shook hands. He had a firm but gentle handshake and Aurora immediately liked him.

'How long have you been working here, Nigel?' she asked.

'A year. The landlord lets me manage the place without too much interference.'

'I've heard some good things about this place and about you.'

'Who from?' he asked smiling, his large eyes expanding.

'Other reporters. They say you've got a good ear for new bands.'

'Well, I don't know about that. I'm a failed musician myself, but I know what I like to listen to and we've been really lucky to get some great people playing here. Listen, Aurora, find yourself a good spot, the left-hand side is probably better for your purposes. I've still got a few things to do before the place gets busy. Nice to meet you.' And he directed one of the bar staff to serve her.

She ordered a tonic water and found a small table and chair in the area Nigel suggested. He was right. The stage slanted into the back of the pub. This wasn't obvious when you first walked in. Aurora sat down and took out her paper pad and pen. She'd discovered very quickly that electronic devices and pubs didn't mix. It was an expensive mistake she wouldn't repeat.

A large chalkboard on the wall listed the acts that were due to appear that evening, so she wrote up her pad in preparation. She soon forgot (or got used to) the stale smell of beer, people and food while she wrote up a description of the pub: peeling wallpaper, patches of baldness where paint should have been, worn carpet. Were those stains or part of the faded carpet pattern? The bar of old wood was probably the original bar and was kept spotlessly clean, but despite this, Aurora noted black burns dotted in random patterns, and in the far corner, a red stain that crept up the wood like rising damp. The pub became busy and crowded.

There was palpable excitement as the first band was setting up. A friend of Nigel's (as Aurora found out later in the evening) was helping the bands out. He had been a roadie in a previous life and enjoyed being able to advise the musicians and help them with changeovers for a few free drinks.

The first act was an acoustic band of three young men, a classical guitar, a double bass and a snare drum. All had short hair and wore black clothes. Aurora tried to dispel her preconceptions of the artists she saw, but it was difficult sometimes, especially when bands would go for a uniform look on stage.

The pub was almost full and people jostled for the few chairs left, moving them to sit with friends and leaving gaps.

Once the band started playing, she closed her eyes and concentrated on the music: sound, lyrics, voice, harmony, tempo and performance.

There were to be five acts that evening and it wasn't a bad start with the first act. They were pleasant and an enjoyable introduction to the evening, but hardly a breathtaking experience. However, Aurora appreciated the difficulties in performing, especially to an indifferent audience. So, she circled the positive words she used in her notes.

After the third act, Nigel took a drink over to her.

'What do you think so far?' he asked.

'Not bad. I've liked all of them, but they're not really getting to me. It'll be a positive review though. Nearly all my comments have been positive.'

Nigel looked over Aurora's pad.

'You wrote all of that?'

'Yes, why?'

'I've never seen any of the reporters write anything down. They just record it and then pan the acts in their reviews.'

'Well, I'm here to listen to live music, so I want to capture what I hear—not a recording. Thanks for the drink.'

'It's on the house,' he replied and rushed back to the bar.

The fourth act took some time to set up. Aurora checked the name: The Forum.

The band were dressed smart casual, wearing jeans and shirts. Except for the lead guitarist, who wore a long grey woollen skirt, big black boots and a dark grey vest which showed off her strong arms. Her brown hair was shaved at the back and sides while the long hair was tied up in a small bun on her head. She wore subtle make-up, browns and burgundies. To Aurora she was the focus of the band. The lead singer was confident and comfortable on stage, his voice strong and passionate. Aurora found herself watching the entire performance. The band was mesmerising and obviously talented. This was the band Aurora had been waiting for. The Forum would be the next big thing, she was sure of it. She couldn't quite place their music; the style and performance changed between the two songs they performed and yet the pieces of performance seemed to build a narrative, a whole. Their performance flowed. They seemed the most naturally talented musicians Aurora had heard in years and she loved the fact that the lead guitarist was a woman. A solid performance with technical ability.

Aurora wanted to speak to the band, but there was one more act left to perform. The final act was usually the act that Nigel rated the best and they were the ones who got the breaks. However, Aurora was not taken by them at all. To her they appeared arrogant and dismissive of the audience, as if they had already achieved their musical success.

Aurora left her table and went in search of The Forum. Nigel was with them. When he saw Aurora coming towards them, he waved her over and introduced them, making a big fuss about the fact that Aurora had listened to the music and taken notes.

Nigel had agreed to them performing the following week, then he rushed back to the bar.

'I'm really pleased to meet you. Your performance was excellent,' shouted Aurora over the music.

'Thanks,' shouted the lead singer. Aurora hadn't caught their names owing to the noise in the pub, so she wrote down:' I'D LIKE TO INTERVIEW YOU.'

The lead singer motioned for them to walk to the back and out into the garden.

'That's better. I'm Brandon. Sorry, I didn't catch your name in there.'

'Aurora, Aurora Beltrame. I'm a music journalist and I'd like to interview you, the band.'

'Nice to meet you, Aurora. Do you want to interview us now? I'm not sure if we have time,' Brandon replied looking at the lead guitarist.

'What about tomorrow? If I hire out a room here? Maybe an hour of your time?'

'Tomorrow works for us. About two?' suggested the lead guitarist.

'Perfect,' replied Aurora ecstatic.

'Can I get your names again? Sorry.'

'I'm Rachel, lead guitar. This is Brandon, lead vocals, that's John on bass guitar and Terry on drums,' said Rachel pointing to each of them, leaving her hand on Terry's arm.

'I really liked your set. Look, I know you've probably got a lot on, so I won't keep you.'

'I'm flattered you want to interview us, but can I ask why?' asked Rachel.

'You're the first band I've seen that really excited me. I've waited for weeks for this to happen. I don't work for a big magazine or anything like that. I have my own blog and I write reviews for the local papers, but this interview would be different. It'll be about you as a band.'

'Could you give us a couple of minutes?' asked Rachel.

'Of course.' Aurora walked back inside the pub and waited by the window. Had she pushed too hard? Seemed too desperate? She needed this break badly. The final act had just finished their set and there was an eruption of cheering, shouting and clapping as the band acknowledged the crowd before making their way to the bar.

Aurora looked back outside and saw Rachel beckon to her.

'Aurora, we would love to do an interview with you. Thanks for your honesty. We'll see you here tomorrow at two. We can't stay too long as we have another gig in Richmond tomorrow night. Actually, would you like to come with us?' Rachel leaned in. 'It's a much nicer venue—but I wouldn't tell Nigel that,' she added with a smile.

'I would love to join you tomorrow,' exclaimed Aurora.

'Good. We'll see you tomorrow then.' Rachel and the others were moving to pack up the rest of their equipment.

'Tomorrow,' repeated Aurora and she leaned forward to shake their hands again.

Aurora passed by the bar, which was heaving with a large crowd surrounding the last act. She just managed to catch Nigel's eye. He beckoned her over and took her into the back of the pub. There was the clattering and hissing from the kitchen with steam escaping into the narrow corridor. Nigel walked past and down to the end of the corridor where he unlocked a dark door. Switching a light on, he encouraged Aurora into a very clean and organised office. There was such a stark difference between the two spaces: the office all white walls, desk, locked cupboards complementing the dark wood parquet floor tiles and framed certificates on the walls. And then the pub out front with all of its worn wood and frayed carpet.

'We can talk properly in here,' said Nigel smiling and indicating a chair for Aurora to sit in.

'I take it you really like The Forum?'

'They're the best musicians I've seen since I started this job. Granted, I haven't been doing this long, but I've seen and heard a lot of performers and The Forum have something more. They have a real presence on stage and their musical ability is incredible. I was hoping I could book a room or space here tomorrow afternoon to interview them?'

'Yeah, of course. We have a function room you can use. Will you mention the pub?'

Aurora smiled.

'Of course. How could I not? Listen, Nigel, you've been more than generous and I really appreciate it. You definitely deserve your reputation.'

'That's kind of you, but it's just part of the job.'

'No, it's more than that. You clearly care about the musicians, about your customers and your team. It's not just the job!'

Aurora was adamant. Nigel was exceptional and Aurora was going to make sure he was recognised. There was no bullshit with Nigel. He was genuinely nice. Aurora suddenly felt emotional, overwhelmed by the kindness and goodness Nigel showed. Was such behaviour so rare that it touched her so deeply? The well of emotion bubbled, filling her chest with a pain she hadn't felt in decades. Was it the kindness of a stranger? The altruism of an acquaintance? Or just that this genuine feeling revealed something good in the world? As mad and illogical as it seemed, it was far more emotional to experience kindness than it was to experience violence. Was this the world we lived in or was it just Aurora's perception of her world? Aurora managed to hold the well back, just.

'Are you OK?' asked Nigel.

'Yes, fine. It's late, I should be going. I'll be here just before two tomorrow.'

'No problem, Aurora. Are you sure you're OK?'

'Yes. Thanks, Nigel.' And Aurora stood up to leave.

As Nigel was locking the office door, Aurora stood facing him. As he turned, he almost walked into her, surprised to find her still standing there.

Aurora put her hand out. Nigel took it and shook it warmly. Aurora held it for just a second longer, looking and feeling for Nigel as a deep understanding passed between them—a deep human connection that surprised and comforted her at the same time. Aurora felt it as a shared experience as they walked down the corridor, enveloped in a warm silence. Aurora gave Nigel one more wave and a smile as she left the pub.

*

Amber hopes her concerns about Harry are just that and there isn't anything concrete behind the change. She tries to speak to Aurora about it, but Aurora dismisses Amber's comments. She and Harry have a special relationship, that is all. Harry responds to her. They share the same tastes. Amber is placated for a while.

Aurora and Harry meet at the Café des Beaux Arts. They love being surrounded by the colourful walls painted in different styles while they drink Moroccan mint tea and chat about music, literature and philosophy. There are bookshelves full of old paperbacks that anyone can take to read. Aurora and Harry pick a book at random to chat through, like a discovery game. Only this time, Harry doesn't want to play. He wants to talk to Aurora. He wants to talk about the concert again and what happened. Aurora talks about Morpheme and the music. She breaks down the rhythm and lyrics. Harry smiles, but his patience is waning. He doesn't want to hear about how creative or amazing Morpheme's music is anymore. To him, the concert is secondary to the event of the evening.

Harry moves around the table to sit next to Aurora on the bench. He looks at her and takes her hand in his. He strokes her hand. Aurora lets him. He is like a puppy that needs affection. He looks into her eyes and for a moment Aurora feels a whisp of fear, like burnt paper that flits through the air and then crackles into invisible soot.

But this is Harry, she says to herself. Harry speaks. Aurora listens. Aurora stiffens. Like a corpse, her life has drained away from her.

*

Aurora is shocked awake by her body panting and screaming silently for air. She is covered in a film of cold sweat, and suddenly a cramp in her calf muscle burns through her and she bites down on the duvet as she tries to focus on her breathing to relax the muscles. The 20 seconds of pain seem to last a lifetime. It is still dark in the bedroom, but as her eyesight adjusts, she can see the furniture outlined in the blue-grey surrounding her. She gets up to fetch a drink of water. Her leg is still in pain, but it is manageable. She is too scared to return to sleep and stays awake watching day take over from night.

*

Aurora arrived ten minutes early, but The Forum were already there. Nigel had settled them into the function room with drinks. Aurora was a little flustered and tired as she realised she wouldn't have time to prepare herself.

'Hello Rachel. Hi guys,' said Aurora as she entered the room. They were all in baggy T-shirts and shorts. The transformation was interesting to Aurora. Here, now, they looked like ordinary people, like teenagers. No indication of the amazing talents that had engaged her so much the previous night.

'There are just a couple of formalities to go through before we start, to protect both parties. In this form you grant consent for me to write about the band. I've restricted this to just the interview questions though and it only relates to this session. The other form, if you don't mind, is permission to take photographs of you while you're performing.' Aurora handed the forms directly to Rachel.

'This feels really official,' said Brandon.

'Well, yes, but you should always get agreements in writing. It saves a lot of trouble later,' replied Aurora.

'John, have a quick read. I'm happy with this. Aurora's right, we need to be sure we agree to things we are happy with. We shouldn't just sign up to anything. Have you got a pen?' she asked Aurora.

'This looks fine to me.' He handed the forms back to Rachel, who signed first and passed it to the others. When Aurora had given them their copies, she sat down with a cup of tea and settled with her pad and a pen on her lap and pressed the record button on her phone.

'So, we can start the interview, unless you have any questions?'

'I feel like I'm in a job interview,' said Brandon laughing. John nudged him.

'No, we don't have any questions, Aurora. Please go ahead,' replied John.

Brandon was still smiling; his eyes betrayed his real intention to have a bit of fun with Aurora.

'How did you come together as a band?'

John, Terry and Brandon looked towards Rachel to answer the question first.

'I couldn't get into a band. I didn't want to be in an all-girl band just because I was female. I wanted to be in a good band, but guys would always get the jobs over me, even when it was clear I was technically better. Some guys just feel really uncomfortable with a girl in the band. I felt like screaming. One day, after another failed audition, I was really depressed. I was sitting in the kitchen with my head on the table, trying not to cry, trying to work out what I should do next, when my little brother comes into the kitchen and sees me at the table. He puts his arm around me and asks me what's wrong. I tell him, and he matter-of-factly says, "Just start your own band." Just like that! And so that's what I did. I advertised like the other bands had and held auditions in the church hall. I met John first. In fact, John, you were the first guy to come to the audition,' said Rachel turning to John.

'I thought it was just like any other audition, but it was a bit strange to see so many girls and women there. I thought I'd got the audition details wrong,' he laughed. 'I talked to Rachel and auditioned for her. We ended up playing together. It seemed so natural; we both seemed to know what was needed in the performance. After the audition we went to get some food and chatted about everything. To be honest, I was in awe of Rachel's guitar playing and still am.

'Then we set up new auditions and met Brandon and Terry. Brandon, you were already with a band at that point?' Rachel indicated that Brandon should respond.

'Yeah, it was shit. They kept playing the same crap all the time, just thrash metal. There was nothing I could do except growl. I felt limited. I kept telling myself that things would develop, the guys would try other things, but they never did. They kept talking about gigs, but they never materialised. I think in six months we played three gigs, and one of those was in the drummer's dad's restaurant. Can you imagine, thrash metal in a restaurant? I was desperate to get out and then I saw the audition. When I met Rachel and John, I signed up as soon as I could. I was just happy to sing in a different way and try new things. I was really lucky they offered me the job. That was, what... a year ago?' asked Brandon.

'Yes, a year. You don't realise how quickly time passes,' replied John.

'And then we met Terry, who auditioned with a snare drum and hi-hat and was incredible,' said Rachel beaming at Terry.

'I can't even remember what I played,' said Terry. Aurora looked up from her pad. It was the first time she had heard Terry speak.

'You played 'Funky Drummer' and 'St. Anger',' said Rachel smiling.

'Oh, yeah. I'd played with a couple of other bands but didn't feel settled, like I belonged. When I met Rachel and John and we talked about music, it was amazing. They were what I was looking for. A group I could contribute to, somewhere I could experiment a little, not just be a drummer in the background. And Rachel understands how my mind works, so if I don't get a song or a section, she writes it down for me,' said Terry squeezing Rachel's hand.

'Now this is a standard question, but always interesting, who are your musical influences?' asked Aurora.

'My main influences are Rachel, John and Terry. I don't think I will ever get an opportunity to work with better musicians or bandmates.'

'Ah, Brandon, that's so nice,' replied Rachel while John nudged Brandon, embarrassed.

'I'm not saying it because it's nice. It's true. I've learnt so much from you. The thing is, I like lots of different styles and music genres, depending on what kind of mood I'm in: opera, soul, jazz, metal, electro, hip-hop, pop, anything, and I love finding music that's different. So being with these guys is great because they have such amazing taste in music and technical ability that they can turn something they've heard into something completely new. They also push me to use my voice in different ways. It's exactly how you want to work as a musician. You want to bounce ideas off each other, you want to have the time and space to try new things, see if they work. If not, park it for later. But no session is wasted,' said Brandon as he turned to John.

'I'd say that my influences stem from my dad. He's a big jazz fan and I really got into Hank Crawford when I started playing the saxophone at school. I think my dad secretly harboured dreams of my becoming a jazz saxophonist. As I got more involved in jazz, I felt a pull towards the double bass so took that up as well. Then I moved onto bass guitar and wanted to see what I could do with that. When I discovered Ennio Morricone, that just changed my life. I know that sounds weird, considering his film and TV work, but he started off with his jazz band and look at the work he's done. It's incredible. For me, the biggest discovery was that instruments should not be confined to genres of music. Any instrument can be used to create any kind of music. Once you work that out, it makes the whole process so much easier because you're not hung up on how it should sound. You go with what sounds good to you, and if it sounds good to you, it's likely to sound good to somebody else out there too.'

'Rachel and Terry are the techies in the band, which helps to rein in our creative spurts. And you need that discipline because you can't use everything you create. You have to be selective to some degree, especially when you're starting out,' said John leaning forward and looking at Rachel.

'You know, I don't think we've ever discussed our influences like this before. It's really interesting listening to John and Brandon talk about their influences like this. In comparison, I think my influences are quite restricted. I like big music: Beethoven, Carl Orff, music that sounds like a thunder storm and gets inside you. From a lead guitar perspective, I would say Yngwie Malmsteen is a huge influence. His technical ability is unsurpassed as far as I'm concerned, and I think he's really underrated. No one knows where to place him exactly. It's like John said, you shouldn't confine instruments to genres, but people do. If you play electric guitar, it can only be rock, metal, or pop. Anything else just seems to jar people.'

'And Terry, who are your influences?'

'I can't name particular people because I like to be myself when I play. But I love the idea of creating different sounds using instruments, and even using everyday objects to create new sounds. Like in *Belleville Rendez-Vous*. I love that film. It's so clever: bicycle wheels, vacuum cleaners and even a newspaper, pure genius. I love listening to animated soundtracks. If you think about it, all the sound in an animated film needs to be created, just as the drawings have to be created. It's a great source of sound. And the imagination that goes into creating sound effects is incredible. While you're watching the film, you think the sound is really made by what you're watching, but in fact it's something completely different making that sound. There's some really exciting sound art being created in Europe at the moment and it's something I would like to explore more—going beyond the music, if you like, the essence of sound.'

'Rachel, what motivates you?' asked Aurora.

'Making music I enjoy and working with these guys. I think we've gelled really well and I want to push myself and the others to see where we can take this.'

'John, what about you?'

'I agree with Rachel. It has to be the music, otherwise we might as well go and get other jobs.'

'Brandon?'

'Um, for me it's the performance. Yes, the music is important, but I want my performance to be great. I want the guys to be happy with it.'

'Terry?'

'The sound. Finding the sound that's different, unique to us as a band. And Rachel motivates me. I want to make her happy,' he replied smiling and blushing.

'OK, two more questions. You're promoting your current album, but are you writing any new material?'

They all leaned forward and looked at each other. Rachel nodded towards John.

'We are writing as ideas come through. At the moment, our focus is on promotion of the current material, getting people to recognise us and our music. Rachel is a really good manager. She makes sure we spend at least one day a week writing, playing, experimenting. It's hard sometimes though when you just want to do nothing, watch TV, read a book, do something else. But we need to keep up the momentum.'

'Last question and thank you for your patience. What do the next few months look like for you?'

'We're working the pub circuit and have bookings for the next couple of months. A bit of travelling around the UK and trying to negotiate some spots at music festivals for the summer. I can give you a list of our dates and venues,' suggested Rachel.

'That would be great. I'll try and include as many of them as I can in the article. 57 minutes. Thanks for your time today,' said Aurora.

'We'd better get going,' said John standing up and stretching his arms.

Nigel knocked on the door. They all called out, 'Come in.'
'All done?'

'Yes, and thanks for the room and the drinks, Nigel,' said Aurora.

'We'll see you next week Nigel,' called out Rachel as they left the room.

Aurora posted the finished interview on her blog with a number of photos of the band the next day. A few social media posts and some online sharing pushed the article into the wider world. Aurora waited with anticipation for the result.

Dialectic

'I can do the seventh, eighth or ninth any time, but before that I'm fully booked,' said Aurora on the phone.

'The ninth at 10.00am. Perfect. We should allow a couple of hours for everything, so we should be finished by lunchtime. Can you email me the hotel details and I'll confirm in writing. They will need to complete and sign the forms I sent through. And *they* need to sign them. The forms won't be accepted if someone signs on their behalf. Thanks. Bye.'

Aurora leaned back in her chair. Another interview booked. She looked at the time. A couple of hours of work and then Jennie would arrive. Aurora focused, finishing an article, arranging photographs, planning the next three interviews and researching the bands.

*

'Oh my God, Aurora, it's so good to see you!' exclaimed Jennie hugging Aurora in the doorway. 'I've missed you,' she added.

'I've missed you too. Come in,' said Aurora still holding onto Jennie's hand as she closed the door. 'The wine is chilling, the takeaway ordered and I'm ready to hear all your news!' she said smiling.

'You've done some decorating since I was here last,' said Jennie looking around the lounge.

'Yes, I needed to create a workspace, so I thought I might as well redecorate while I was at it. I hadn't realised how much control David had over my life until I started thinking about what I wanted: colour, furniture, style. I hadn't even noticed how restricted my environment was. Anyway, how do you like it?'

'This is definitely you, Aurora. I love the colours and the industrial look. Dare I say it... 80s,' said Jennie smiling.

'Is it really that obvious?' laughed Aurora.

'So, tell me, how are you and Mike doing?' Aurora asked as she poured out the chilled Muscadet into two glasses.

'We're well, thanks,' replied Jennie, hesitating for a second.

'I realised what you were trying to do when we were talking in the café and you were defending Mike. To be honest, it pissed me off at the time. I was convinced you didn't take my concerns seriously. I couldn't help myself and had a go at Mike that night. We had a big argument, but it cleared the air.'

'Was it about the calls?'

'Well, that was how it started, but as we continued to argue, I realised that wasn't the real issue,' said Jennie quietly.

'What was it, Jennie? You don't have to tell me if you don't want to.'

'I feel I should tell you. I owe you. It was about sex. I was getting bored. I mean sitting down to dinner every night at the same time is fine, but I don't want to book in my sex sessions as well! I want spontaneity. I want lust, I want Mike to take me away from the washing-up and make love to me on the kitchen floor, rubber gloves and all,' said Jennie pleadingly.

'What did Mike say?'

'He agreed. He found our sex life boring too, but he swore all the calls and overtime were work-related and that he wasn't seeing anyone else. Can you believe it? He thought I wanted scheduled sex, so he didn't say anything! We had the best sex we'd ever had that night,' Jennie said grinning.

'How was the holiday?' asked Aurora.

'Wonderful! Mike had gone all out. That was when he explained that all the extra hours he'd been doing was to pay for the holiday. I felt really bad then. You tried to tell me. I'm so glad you convinced me to go ahead with the holiday,' said Jennie sipping her wine.

'I knew Mike wanted it to be a special holiday for you. I did panic a little when you started saying you wouldn't go on the holiday. I'm really pleased you've worked things out with him. I keep telling you he's a great guy. There aren't that many of them about. You need to keep him. Trust me on this, I know from experience.'

'I know. And I know I should listen to you,' said Jennie looking into her glass.

'You know what I'm like, I just find it hard to take on board other people's advice,' she laughed. 'Well, what have you been up to?'

Just then the doorbell rang.

'Dinner,' said Aurora as she brought in the takeaway and started laying it out on the side table she had brought out of the cupboard.

They settled into their meal, enjoying the food they shared.

'So?' asked Jennie.

'I can't believe how different things are now. When I think about what I was doing this time last year! Working on my own projects has been hard, trying to anticipate what other people want and need: contracts, insurance, permissions. Always chasing the next job. It was hard in the beginning, but now the work is coming to me. That makes me feel good. I feel I've achieved something.'

'Are you happy though?'

'Ecstatic! I know it doesn't sound like it, but I'm trying to stay in control and not get over-excited. I'm just nervous the bubble might burst. Sometimes I find myself staring out of the window and wanting to run away, to disappear. Really disappear, fade into oblivion while I'm in this good spot.'

'Don't think like that. Enjoy it, make the most of what you've built up and live it. You're the only person who has made this happen. No one else can take that away from you,' said Jennie leaning towards Aurora, looking straight into her face.

'I'm just worried I'll end up sabotaging myself. Sometimes I feel an urge to drop everything—no work, no contacts—destroy it all to see where I could end up. I know. It's shocking to you that I would think like that. I guess it's because I'm in full control over everything I do now. When we worked at NSM, I was working to someone else's plans, ideas, drives. The motivation is the same though. You do your best because you want recognition for what you do. That was my motivation. Definitely. The thought of doing something wrong or messing up never even entered my mind. But it does now that I'm working for myself. I think it's because the responsibility lies with me, so the power also lies with me. And sometimes that feels like I should destroy it.' Aurora looked down at her plate and placed it on the table. She'd eaten enough.

'Don't blow it,' said Jennie. 'Why would you make your life harder than it needs to be? I don't understand why you would think like that?'

'It's not deliberate. I don't know. Maybe it's depression? You know, the strangest thing about this experience is that I used to dream about having a life like this, then I'd get up and go to work in the real world. Now I feel like I'm living in a dream world, there is no reality for me and it's a little scary. I feel trapped, sometimes.'

'Aurora, you need to snap out of this. You *are* living in the real world; it's just a different reality. Don't jeopardise what you've built up. I would love to have your life, but I don't have the talent or knowledge to do something like this. No, let me finish. It's not only that. I don't want to change; I like working for an organisation, having that structure and support. So, while I wish I had your life, it would scare me too much to even think about trying. But you've done it. You have that drive and ability to know what needs to be done and how to do it. You showed that at NSM. This life is you. You were always going to do something different. Don't disappoint me on this.'

'I never thought we'd be having this kind of conversation together,' laughed Aurora.

'Don't ignore what I've said, Aurora. You need to take it seriously. I will always be honest with you and I'm privileged you've been honest with me, but you need to take what I've said to you seriously,' said Jennie curtly.

'I'm sorry, Jennie. I didn't mean to dismiss what you said. I promise, I am listening to you. Next time I have these thoughts, I'll think of you,' smiled Aurora moving forward to hug Jennie.

When had their relationship changed? Or maybe it hadn't changed? It was just that Aurora had never taken Jennie seriously enough as a real friend. She suddenly felt a gaping hole inside her. Was she that shallow? Had she dismissed Jennie as just a work colleague, someone to catch up with, but not to take into her confidence? And yet here they were discussing their most intimate thoughts and emotions. Aurora felt the ground shifting underneath her. The shifting dreamscape that her life had become disorientated her.

'So, tell me about what you've been working on and what happened with that band?'

Aurora had to pull herself out of the mental maze. She smiled at Jennie, hoping she would think she'd snapped out of her mood. Was that dishonest?

'I told you about The Forum, didn't I?' she asked trying to inject some energy into her voice.

'Yes, you told me about the first interview with them.'

'Well, they're signed up with a record label and due to start a European tour soon. You must have heard their new single, 'Get it Right'. It's all over YouTube and various music shows.'

'Is that them?' asked Jennie surprised.

'Yes, that's them and they've asked me to work on a book with them when they return from their tour.'

'See what I mean, Aurora? You just have that amazing ability to make things happen.'

Aurora wanted to say, 'But it doesn't feel like that to me', but instead she said, 'I'm really pleased for them. They are so lovely and talented, and they made my job easy. And it's thanks to them that I now have so much work coming in. I won't bore you with the names, but I've got interviews with some big bands now.'

'Is there any one band or singer you really want to interview?' asked Jennie.

'Well, yes there are a few, mainly from my teenage years.'

'What about a band you *wouldn't* want to interview?'

'That's easy: Morpheme. Do you remember them?'

'Yes, I remember their later music. I can't say I was a fan though, not my kind of music. Why wouldn't you want to interview them?'

'Because it would be too personal for me. I was, am, a huge fan, so it would be a disaster.'

'I would never have put you into that music category. That's interesting,' said Jennie looking a little bewildered. Had her perception of Aurora shifted?

'Yes, I was into a lot of different things in those days—pre-David.'

'What is it about Morpheme you like so much?'

'I like their music, the early days when they first broke through. Their music was energetic, the songs painful and the sounds experimental. I don't think I would have explained it quite like that when I was 17, but that's the best way to explain my passion for them now. And when I saw them live at Hammersmith, it was incredible. The performance was intimate, personal and astounding. Their music sounded different to me after seeing them live. They lived their music and I think it was then I felt I had a connection with them. But all fans feel that. The music brings you together, but then the connection goes beyond that.'

'You sound like one of those obsessive fans.'

'I guess I am in a way. After my split from David, I started looking through all my stuff again and found my CDs, concert programmes, T-shirts, all this stuff from my teens I thought David had thrown out. Going through all of that brought back those memories and feelings I had at the time.

Not just about the band, but stuff at college as well. It took me back to that girl who had so many dreams and ambitions, wanted to have fun and do things with her life. I wanted an opportunity to go back to her, and Morpheme enabled that. So, while I am a fan and would love to meet them, I'm not sure that I would interview them well. My personal feelings about them would get in the way. And that is the weirdest thing because they have no idea about the impact they've had on my life.'

'I never understood fans like that, those girls who would camp outside singers' houses and follow them everywhere, including going to all their concerts as if by some miracle the guy would turn around to them and propose and they'd live happily ever after. You weren't one of those, were you?' asked Jennie.

'Uh, no. I wasn't that obsessed. My feelings were kept in check.' Aurora smiled. 'Anyway, I've got plenty of work to keep me going for the next few months without having to worry about making a fool of myself in front of Morpheme.'

'Are you planning a holiday at any point?' asked Jennie.

'Can't even begin to think about that yet, let alone plan it. If I can get this book deal, then I can probably start to think about a break, but I need to keep busy, keep up the momentum,' replied Aurora. That was the dichotomy in her life: build or obliterate.

'Well, what about coming over to our place for a weekend? We can have a barbecue, take a picnic over to Kenwood?' asked Jennie excited.

'I'd love to, but a lot of my work is done over weekends. What about you and Mike joining me at one of the venues instead? We can eat an early dinner and then go onto the club?'

'Mike would love that! But I will hold you to coming over to our place for a break. You can't just work all the time.' Then she added, 'Well, I think I've eaten way too much here. I'm going to struggle to get home,' she said doing up her belt.

'Are you going already?'

'It's half eleven. I should have been home by now,' said Jennie looking at her phone. 'Look, Mike's worried. Do you mind if I call him?'

'Go ahead,' said Aurora taking the dishes into the kitchen.

'Mike's coming to pick me up. I can have a final glass of wine.'

'Thanks for coming over, I've really enjoyed this evening, Jennie.'

'So have I. Just don't disappear like that again, OK?'

'I won't. I promise to keep in touch. I'll come downstairs with you and say hi to Mike when he arrives.'

The night was dark and dry. The unseasonal warmth of the day had dissipated into the chilly night. A car's headlights crept towards them as they stood outside Aurora's block of flats. Jennie recognised the car and walked towards it. Aurora followed her. Once Jennie was seated, Aurora bent down to see into the car.

'Hi Mike. How are you?'

'Hi Aurora. Good, thanks. You?'

'Better for tonight,' she smiled.

'I won't ask what you've been chatting about. When are we going to see you at our place?'

'Soon, soon. Jennie will organise it. I've invited you both to join me one night at a club. We'll sort out dates and times.'

'Really? That sounds great. I can't remember the last time I saw a live band,' replied Mike leaning right over Jennie.

'I told you he'd get excited,' laughed Jennie pushing him back.

'I'll call you,' said Aurora.

Jennie and Mike drove away, leaving Aurora standing in the cold, dark night.

From the blackness, a car's headlights smothered Aurora in its bright light. She couldn't see the car or the driver, but the situation felt eerie to her and she rushed back into her block as the car sped away down the road.

*

Back in her flat Aurora felt safe. The stale smell of takeaway food and wine still lingered and she opened a window. The episode with the car had shaken her. She didn't know why. Agitated, she cleaned and washed up in the kitchen. She had really enjoyed her evening with Jennie. It had been a long time since she'd been as open with anyone and it felt good. Having tidied up, she looked around the lounge, seeing her things, her tastes, her personality reflected in the room. She looked at her workspace, the work board, the computer, the magazine boxes, the CDs, the Maya Green jazz painting. This was her space and it reflected her new life.

Jennie was right of course. Aurora was mad to let her insecurities derail what she had achieved. Tiredness crept upon her. As soon as she lay down, she fell into a deep sleep.

*

Aurora cannot comprehend what Harry is telling her. He is cutting through their connection, dividing them forever. She asks Harry to stop. But now that he is on this path, he cannot. He is committed to taking this to the end. He wants to take their relationship to the next stage. He loves Aurora. He wants her. She is flattered, but she loves him as a friend, a brother. There is nowhere else for their relationship to go. Can they not just remain friends? This is no longer an option Harry can live with. He realised at the Morpheme concert that he loves Aurora; that he needs her in every way. She has been a safe haven, an escape room, a literal lifeline for him and this manifestation of his love for her only grows stronger. Aurora wants to leave. She is taunted with stress as her mind races through objections and alternatives to Harry's request. With every objection, Harry counters with a rational argument. Aurora cannot win this argument with Harry. She wants passion, he gives her rationality. She wants soft touches. He wants to possess her.

To escape his claustrophobic grip, she agrees to a trial period of dating. But he must agree to let her go if it doesn't work out. Harry agrees and seals the deal with a hug and a request to take her out the next evening.

Aurora makes the most of this new development and decides she owes it to Harry to make an effort. She buys a new black skirt, matching it with a red shirt and black jacket. She thinks through the best way to manage Harry's contact. Before the barrier, Aurora was comfortable hugging and holding Harry. Now she feels something else.

They agree to meet at Café des Beaux Arts. The evenings are full of poetry and jazz. Aurora finds a table at the far end, away from the noisy bar. She orders a tonic water while waiting. The poetry acts are good this evening, only she won't remember them.

Aurora looks at her watch. She has finished her drink. Harry is never late.

Discovery

'Hello?'

'Delivery for Aurora Beltrame.'

'OK, thank you.' Aurora pressed the buzzer. She waited for a knock at her flat door.

'Delivery.' Aurora opened the door.

'Thank you,' she said and the delivery guy was gone.

She was left with a large upright box. She looked into the slot and saw what she thought were petals. The name and address were correct, but she had no idea who could have sent the flowers. Oh, maybe it was The Forum? A thank you.

Aurora brought the box into her flat, excited by the surprise delivery.

She pulled out the vase of red and white roses. They were beautiful, but it struck her these were not the choice of flower from acquaintances or friends. A card was stuck on a clip in front of the roses, large and mismatched with the elegance of the flowers. A creeping dread overtook her, the sharp thorns and leaves of the roses gaining prominence over the petals. She unclipped the card and opened it.

I MISS YOU!
XX

This was a mistake surely? Her phone was ringing. Still in shock, Aurora answered it.

'How do you like the flowers?' It was the voice she feared hearing again.

Aurora wanted to throw the phone away, but she knew she had to deal with this shit.

'Why are you calling me?'

'What! I can't call my ex-wife after sending her flowers?'

'Why are you sending me flowers, David?' Aurora asked angrily.

'You can't have forgotten. It's our anniversary.' Aurora could hear him smile as he said it.

'We're divorced. There is no anniversary.'

'OK, well, call it a peace offering then.'

'Don't call me, David. We're divorced, finished. I don't want anything to do with you,' Aurora said, angry at him for forcing her into a defensive position.

'I'm sorry. Just give me a couple of minutes to explain,' he said feigning desperation. The old routine. 'You owe me that after all the years we've been together.'

'I don't owe you anything, David. What is it?'

'I saw your name come up on some online articles. I just wanted to ask how the new career was going?'

'Ahh, that's it, is it? You want to sniff around my new career, see if there's an angle for you? Well, there isn't. There is nothing for you.'

'Not even for old times' sake?' The malice was unmistakeable.

'Fuck off, David. You don't own me and you can't control me anymore and if you don't leave me alone, I will go to the police.'

'You wouldn't do that to me? I'm concerned about you, that's all. Look, can we just meet for dinner? Where's the harm in that?'

'David, I don't know how else to say this, but NO. We are divorced and we got divorced for one reason.'

'You wanted the divorce, not me.'

'No, you didn't, because you were controlling my life. And then you delayed making the payments even after the court threatened you with prison. That was my money, David. And now you act as if nothing happened. Well, it did happen. A lot happened!'

'I'm sorry, I just need to talk to someone. I do miss you, you know. I still love you.' The other tactic.

'Is this what you wanted to talk about?'

'I just thought, now that some time has passed, you might have mellowed.'

Aurora was so angry she would have punched David in the face had he been standing in front of her.

'Don't call me again. If you do, or if I receive anything in the post—deliveries, emails, anything—I will report you to the police for harassment.' And she ended the call, throwing the phone onto the sofa.

She was trembling. She wanted to punch something, kick something, throttle the lack of control that she felt until it was beaten into nothing. David's behaviour outlined a very real fear she had about what he was capable of. She sat down on the sofa. Her phone lay next to her like a black stain. How different could 24 hours be? She pulled her cardigan on and wrapped it tightly around her, her arms now stiff and defensive. She wanted to destroy the flowers and the card, but she couldn't. The divorce had shown David was capable of the most manipulative and malevolent behaviours to get what he wanted. She could not, *would* not trust him again.

How dare he lay claim to her, like some chattel? As if some roses would undo all the lies, stealing, cheating, controlling, bullying, mindfucking he had done to her over the years.

She was free of him now and would stay that way. She went into the kitchen. There was still a bottle of red wine left from the previous night with Jennie. She poured herself a large glass, holding the bottle with both hands so she wouldn't spill it, and gulped it down. Her head began to swim and she grabbed a stool to sit down before she fell down.

Aurora felt her world shift again as an unreality took over her life at that moment. That disjointed feeling returned, making her feel unhinged, broken, distant from humanity. Why was life so hard to work out? The divorce should have been the end of her involvement with David, but she felt a deep nausea, a feeling she hadn't felt for so long. David was up to something. What that was she had no idea, but she felt the sickness from the past rise up in her as she ran to the bathroom.

*

David's call had frozen Aurora's ability to concentrate on her work. She had tasks she could complete as routine, but she needed to meet people, needed to immerse herself in other worlds. She had to get out of her flat. Her throat tightened as if it was swelling up, her appetite abandoned her, leaving a horrible aftertaste in her mouth, and her guts felt entangled in some psychosomatic net. She felt she had to escape to another place, another emotion. She didn't want to worry her parents. Maybe David would leave her alone now?

It had been such a long time since Aurora had done anything that wasn't work-related, so she decided it was time to do something. She arranged to meet Jacqui at Green Park. She planned a couple of hours with her and then a visit to the Tate Britain for the 'The Manifesto of Surrealism' exhibition. It had been an age since she had visited an exhibition or the theatre. She hadn't seen Jacqui since 'that episode'. There had been a few worrying phone calls, but Jacqui had persevered and managed to get a new job. That was when Aurora decided her responsibility for her ended. She had her own issues to contend with, and while she wanted to escape her own reality, she wasn't sure meeting with Jacqui would bring about that shift for her. It wasn't until she saw her that she realised she really wanted this time to herself, to explore another reality alone. A completely selfish impulse that only grew as Jacqui recognised Aurora and walked towards her all smiling and pleased to be meeting up. Aurora forced herself to smile and took in a deep breath as she walked towards Jacqui, who almost ran up to her and hugged her. Aurora was taken aback and felt ashamed.

'I was so pleased to get your call, Aurora. I felt embarrassed about what happened, about what you had to see, and how I reacted. I always thought I was stronger than that, that I could get through episodes like that. I really appreciate what you've done for me,' she garbled. 'And how are you? Jennie said you were doing really well in your new job and doing all sorts of exciting things. Well, you're lucky, you see, you got a break. Most of us don't,' Jacqui added as she smiled at Aurora.

'I'm good. Yes, the career change has worked for me, but it's been hard work as well. I probably work more hours now than I did at NSM,' Aurora defended herself. She had forgotten how Jacqui could be so emotionally demanding. God, two hours to go. What had she been thinking? Dealing with personalities was exhausting. Give her twelve-hour days chasing after interviews and researching bands any day. She was suddenly very grateful for her job.

'I won't forget what you did for me. I really don't know what would have happened had you not come over and stayed with me. No one else was there for me in that way. Whether it was embarrassment or just uncertainty about how to handle the situation. But you were there for me, and I knew then that I could rely on you completely.'

Aurora's heart sank. She didn't want anyone to rely on her completely. How could anyone expect such a thing from another human being?

'I don't know if Jennie told you, I'm at Robinson & Hargreaves LLC. I wasn't happy at first because the position was an administrator role, but I have some news and you'll be so proud of me!' Jacqui exclaimed looking like a child with the biggest surprise in the world. 'I've just been made business manager, with my own team and list of clients!'

'Wow, Jacqui, that's wonderful news! Congratulations! When did this happen?' asked Aurora, relieved there was some good news to talk about.

'The role came up last month as the previous manager (I didn't really like her) left. I wasn't sure what to do, I had been an administrator there for six months by that point and passed my probation. I wasn't happy, but didn't want to risk going to a new place. So, I thought about you and what you would do.'

'And what was that?' asked Aurora waiting for Jacqui to explain what she meant.

'Well, all that training you sent us on. I did exactly what you said: SWOT analysis, breakdown of my skills and experience. Don't laugh, but I even did some interview practice in the mirror,' she laughed. 'You're not to tell anyone that!' Jacqui added smiling.

'And they gave you the job. That is really great news.'

'I felt so useless and abandoned when we were made redundant, but you really did make a difference. The whole team feels that. I know you've been in touch with the others as well, checking on us, making sure we had jobs and were OK. Don't brush it off like it is nothing. It means everything to us.' Jacqui lowered her head. 'I'm just sorry I wasn't there for you. I'm sorry I was so selfish as to only think of myself. I was just so caught up in the moment, I couldn't see any future for me and that was all.'

'Don't apologise, Jacqui. It was hard on all of us. I'm just really pleased you're happy now,' said Aurora relaxing as she realised Jacqui would not need her now.

'So, tell me all your news,' said Jacqui.

*

The two hours had come and gone much quicker than Aurora expected. Suddenly, she was at the exhibition and in her element, enjoying the surrealist artwork. Her excursion had worked, pulling her away from the anxiety David had caused her.

Oh, how she had missed these cultural expeditions. It was such a balm on the soul. Aurora felt her body relax and a warmth spread through her chest. This feeling was unlike any other. It was only related to those moments of aesthetic pleasure; and rare those were.

As she was walking through the surrealist exhibition, she stopped at Matta's *The Vertigo of Eros*, a painting so full of strange colourings, content and meaning it required a significant amount of time to stand and take in the work. She was fascinated by its colours fading in and out of each other, its contrasting images, swirls and patterns scratched into the paint, and rhombuses compartmentalising thoughts and expressions. An incredible piece of work.

'What do you like about it?' a rough voice asked behind her. She didn't turn around, thinking the voice must be speaking to someone else.

She felt someone come close to her, and a hand came into view on her left side.

'I was asking what you like about this work?' asked a man. Aurora looked at him, unable to grasp why he was asking her this question. She looked closer. A ripple of reminiscence flowed from the stranger, whose voice recalled a past experience.

She took him in: about six-foot tall, slim build, black but greying hair cut shortish with a nineties' flair on top giving him a boyish look. Blue eyes and an angular jaw supporting a wide head. Not unattractive, but he had a distant look as if was trying to see through Aurora, beyond her. He was dressed in black trousers, a pale blue T-shirt and black tailored jacket. A purple scarf wound its way around his throat. He had the look of someone confident in himself and yet unsure of the world around him. The ripple subsided as Aurora tried to think of a response.

'Are you talking to me?' she asked, just to make sure.

'Yeah, I'm curious. You've been standing at this piece for over 30 minutes and I'm fascinated by what you're seeing,' he said earnestly as if he needed an answer from Aurora.

'Oh, I didn't realise I was standing here that long. Sorry. Was I blocking your view?' Aurora was confused by this man.

'I'm not criticising you. I'd just like to know your opinion. What do you think of it?' he said smiling, his voice softer, deeper.

And then the ripple transformed into a tidal wave of recognition that smacked her out of herself. That voice. And now she could see him! It was Oliver from Morpheme!

Aurora felt dizzy, her blood splashed out of her, leaving only a hollow shell ready to shatter. Oliver asked her if she was OK, but Aurora could only hold her head, and just as she was about to keel over, a guard came and helped Oliver to move Aurora to a bench. They lay her out on the bench with her legs up on the hand rest and slowly Aurora regained consciousness, returning from the fuzzy blackness that had smothered her. She heard voices, his voice. *Oh God!* She thought, *it really is him.* She tried to sit up, into a less embarrassing position. The guard offered her some water and was suggesting some fresh air when

Aurora's nose started bleeding. Red drops splashed the gallery floor. She scrambled for a tissue in her pocket, found one and held it to her nose. Conscious of the mess she was making, she looked for another, but Oliver was already there wiping her blood away with a towel brought by the guard.

A first aid member of staff came over and took Aurora out to a quiet room where she could rest. Oliver was there. Why was he here? The first aider, a young woman with a pony tail and large blue eyes, asked Aurora if she wanted a coffee or tea. Aurora confirmed a black tea with sugar. She felt bleached of all colour and substance. The girl went out saying to Oliver, 'Would you like a tea as well? I'll be back soon to look after your wife.'

'No thanks,' he replied smiling.

Every time he spoke, Aurora felt jerked and pummelled by his voice. Her teenage crush, her love of his music, his voice, his performance all raced back into her heart and mind making her feel ill again. But it was so instant, so overwhelming that Aurora felt she was in a tidal storm, constantly crashing against walls of recognition and battered by memories. Her nosebleed worsened.

Oliver handed her some more tissues.

'Are you OK?' he asked gently.

'Um, yes,' lied Aurora in a muffled voice. 'You really don't have to stay,' she said. But she did want him to stay.

'I'm not leaving you. It's my fault, I must have scared you. I'm really sorry.'

'I don't know what came over me. I was, am, a jerk,' he said quietly.

The young woman returned with two teas, one for Aurora and the other for Oliver. Aurora was both grateful and fretful as it meant Oliver would stay longer and see her in this state. Why didn't she just faint completely; it would have been far less embarrassing. But she just couldn't tear herself away from him. He was here next to her, drinking tea and making sure she was OK.

'Your wife will be alright soon, once she has had something to drink. It can get quite hot in those rooms,' said the smiling young woman to Oliver.

Aurora set her cup down and put her head between her knees, letting out an uncontrolled groan.

'Thank you for your kindness,' said Oliver to the woman. 'My wife does get these turns every now and again. I'm sure she'll be fine.' And turning to Aurora he said, 'We'll go home as soon as you feel you can stand up. I'll look after you, darling.'

Aurora sipped the hot tea, grateful for something to do. Her nose was drying up and she concentrated on her breathing. Whatever Oliver was playing at, she needed to be able to get herself home.

'Could you give me five minutes? I just remembered something. I'll be back shortly!' Oliver said to the woman. She smiled and patted Aurora on the back.

Unsure of what to say or do, Aurora finished her tea and tried to clean herself up. The woman took her to the bathroom, unwilling to let Aurora go on her own. Looking in the mirror Aurora saw her nose and mouth caked in blood. What a sight! Could a chance meeting with your music hero have gone any worse? She cleaned herself up, washed her hands, brushed her hair and applied her favourite hand cream, which was scented with bergamot and rose. The perfume brought her back to herself. In that scent she recognised the woman she was: confident, articulate and professional.

When they returned, Oliver was standing in the room with a bag.

'Your wife seems much better now,' said the first aider, and turning to Aurora she added, 'Look after yourself, get some rest.'

Aurora looked at Oliver expectantly while he played this charade. He took Aurora's hand in his and they walked towards the exit of the building.

*

The chilly wind by the river helped revive Aurora, although she insisted on sitting down on a bench before talking to Oliver.

'I bought you this,' said Oliver, 'as an apology.'

Aurora looked in the bag. She pulled out a large book about the surrealist exhibition.

'But I can't accept this, it's too much,' she said putting the book back in the bag.

'It's not enough. If there is anything else I can do to apologise, please say so. Can I buy you dinner?' he asked imploringly.

Aurora was taken aback. Oliver seemed to her to be two different people: his confident, creative, seductive self and then this other self that was mischievous and capricious.

'Why did you pretend you were my husband?' asked Aurora seriously. The phrase tickled her as she said it, but she had to be serious with Oliver.

'Well, I didn't want to disillusion the poor girl and…'

'And?'

'And I didn't want to leave you in that state. I felt… feel, really bad about it.'

'I need to tell you something,' said Aurora.

'I didn't faint because of what you said or how you said it. I fainted because I suddenly recognised you as the lead singer of Morpheme, one of my favourite bands. There you were standing so close to me and I just couldn't cope with the shock.'

'Only *one* of your favourite bands?' asked Oliver smiling.

'I'm not surprised you've been in so much trouble with other people. You just can't help yourself,' replied Aurora feeling her confidence returning.

'So, can I take you to dinner?' persisted Oliver with a grin.

'What, now?'

'Well, it's after five, is it too early?'

'No, it's just that I'd like to go home and freshen up a bit. I still have blood on my clothes.'

'I didn't notice,' said Oliver looking disappointed.

'I think I need to have a quiet night; I've had way too much excitement for one day. Can we meet for dinner tomorrow?' asked Aurora. Better to delay and get her thoughts and feelings in order.

'What time tomorrow?'

'About six?'

'Can I take your number?'

'Yes.' Aurora was relieved. Oliver seemed disappointed, but it was best this way. She typed her number into his phone.

'Where do you live?' he asked her.

'Near Southgate, North London. What about you?'

'What! You don't know?' That glimmer in his eye.

'Well, I, no, I was just being polite. I don't want you to think I'm one of those stalking fans.'

'I know you're not. You're not on the list.'

'Really? You have a list of stalkers?'

'No, I was joking. I'll book a restaurant near you. What kind of food do you like?'

'Italian, Chinese, Thai, Indian. I don't mind really.'

'I'll call you tomorrow to confirm the details. How are you feeling?'

'Better, thank you. I'm going to get going. It'll take me a while to get home from here.'

'You're coming with me, young lady.'

'Where?'

'You can't go home alone. I'm getting you a taxi.'

'Honestly, I'll be fine on the tube.'

'Let me do this for you. I would never forgive myself if something happened to you on the way home.'

'Why am I agreeing to everything you say?'

'Well, you haven't agreed. I've made concessions, remember? Dinner tomorrow.'

They walked up Millbank and Oliver hailed a black taxi.

Aurora's phone pinged as she climbed into it. She looked at her phone.

'I wanted to make sure you didn't disappear on me.' Oliver winked.

'Please take this lady home and make sure she gets safely to her door. Oh, and charge it to my account,' he said to the driver, tapping his card on the reader. 'I'll see you tomorrow,' he said to Aurora before closing the door. And he waved to her as the taxi U-turned and drove away. The book was lying next to her.

Dinner

Aurora was in a state. She couldn't find anything decent to wear. She flipped from business shirt and trousers to satin dress, from off-the-shoulder to above the knee, from stockings to padded bra. Why was she getting herself into such a state? This wasn't a date; it was an apology dinner.

Sorry for what? Yesterday wasn't his fault. It had just been a shock. Aurora was still panting, breathing hard when she realised who she had been talking to, who she'd spent an afternoon with. Oliver of Morpheme! And he had stayed with her. He had made sure she was OK, got her home safely and sent her a message checking she was alright. He had bought her a book and made her dream come true in the most implausible way. What did he have to be sorry about? Aurora hated this out-of-control feeling. Everything was upside down and turned inside out. She felt like her insides should be on a canvas, an outline of her head with fireworks and waterfalls. A tug of war being played out between her ears with Morpheme on one side and The Forum on the other. Forget-me-nots surrounding her head and repeating patterns of knots: ribbons, ropes, string, laces, straps, all splashed across everything. Arghhh!

She grabbed her bag and went shopping.

*

A taxi came for Aurora to take her to the restaurant. Oliver had chosen well. It was a high-end Italian that she had visited only once before because the prices prohibited frequent visits. The food was excellent. She had returned from her shopping trip with only an hour to shower and change. Deciding on feminine and safe, she went for a dark purple skirt suit and a cream billowy blouse buttoned up to her throat. The look was conservative, suiting her mood. If she went with a work mindset, she'd be able to relax as if it was just another musician she was interviewing. She told herself she had a deadline to meet. Taking a deep breath, she entered the restaurant, her hands trembling as she pulled the door towards her.

Oliver was already seated. He stood up as soon as he saw Aurora approach with the waitress. Aurora smiled but felt her guts empty into a void. She felt sick. She was sweating, her palms were damp and her back dripping. She took off her jacket and quickly wiped her hands to try and dry them off.

Oliver held out his hand to Aurora. She gulped as she took his hand. *Please don't let him feel me trembling*. He took her hand in his and squeezed both of his gently around hers.

'You look amazing! So different from yesterday.' Then he added hastily, 'I mean, you don't look pale; you have plenty of colour in your cheeks today.' And he smiled.

'Would you like to order drinks?' asked the waitress.

Oliver looked at Aurora.

'San Pellegrino water with lemon, no ice, thank you,' requested Aurora. Something to focus on.

'Any wine?'

'No, thank you.'

'Sir?'

'Still water and a bottle of the Château l'Arrosee Saint-Émilion Grand Cru Classé, please.'

'Very good.'

'I hope you approve of the restaurant,' said Oliver.

'I do. I've eaten here once before. The food is excellent.'

'Really? It's my favourite restaurant. I eat here every opportunity I get.'

'Thank you for sending the taxi. It was very considerate of you, but you must let me pay for dinner. You've already been so generous,' said Aurora, wiping her hands on her skirt. When was that water coming?

'No, I invited you,' said Oliver turning his straight face into a smile.

Aurora sighed. She didn't mean to seem ungrateful, but she was so anxious. Breathe, work, think, questions, focus.

'Are you writing any new material?' she asked trying to smile.

'I am. But it's not really working on new material as such. I just want to run with the music and see what happens. It's great to be able to run off on tangents and hear the result. That's not something you can do when you have deadlines,' laughed Oliver.

The waitress brought the drinks and Aurora sipped the cool carbonated water gratefully.

The waitress poured wine into Aurora's glass before she could protest. She didn't want to drink. Then the waitress asked for their order, so they looked at the menu quickly. Aurora skimmed it. Main only. Easy to eat. Spoon.

'Cannelloni,' she ordered.

'I'll have the grilled chicken with green beans and potatoes,' said Oliver. Then after the waitress had left, he whispered to Aurora over the table, 'I promise myself I'll try something different when I come here, but I just love the way they cook the chicken and potatoes here.'

Aurora smiled awkwardly.

'What do you do for a living?' asked Oliver.

'I'm, I was, an actuary manager only last year, but now I'm a music journalist-cum-writer -cum-reporter. I tend to cover new and up-and-coming bands. I wrote the article about The Forum in *NME*,' smiled Aurora now on familiar territory.

'I read that interview. That was you?' asked Oliver surprised.

Aurora wished he wouldn't smile like that; she couldn't look at him. She focused on the table behind him.

'Yes, that was me,' she replied.

'Wow, that was the interview that got them signed up. You're pretty good at that. You said last year you were an actuary manager?' He looked confused.

'Well, you know, you have dreams and career aspirations, but you end up taking another route and then life gets in the way, things happen and you're so far away from doing what you wanted to do and being the person you wanted to be that it seems impossible to find yourself again. I've spent most of my working life in insurance and finance. A big change, huh?'

Oliver was staring at Aurora, searching her eyes, searching for something. Aurora shifted in her seat and looked away to see the waitress bringing their order. She placed their plates and dishes on the table. Aurora was grateful for the additional obstructions and diversions.

'Enjoy,' said Oliver tucking into his chicken.

Aurora carefully dissected her cannelloni with her spoon. She was grateful for the distraction.

'Did you enjoy working with The Forum?' asked Oliver. Aurora looked up.

'Yes, I did. I like the band. We got on from the first time we met at the Dog and Duck pub. They work hard, are considerate and are just nice people. More than anything, I wanted to help them and support them in their success. I felt very strongly that they deserved a break. I worked really hard to get that for them. Now they always put me forward for new work and get me involved in promotions for the band. It's just great to have that trust with them. I can't say I ever felt like that working in the finance sector. How did *you* feel about going on tour?' she then asked, deflecting attention from herself.

'Is that a journalist question or a personal question?' asked Oliver. That spark in his eyes. Was he being serious or setting her up?

'You're safe. I'm not getting paid for this. Personal,' replied Aurora. Had she really said that?

'The first tour we did was fantastic. We didn't know what to expect. We were young, had energy, we didn't listen to advice and we just dived in. The later tours were hard. Deadlines, continuously performing the same material, no breaks, the same fans. You get to the point where you just want to punch everyone in the face, and everyone feels the same way about you. We weren't the first band to split after a world tour and we won't be the last. You know, it's a lot to ask of a small group of people to continuously give of themselves to so many. I kinda wished we'd had someone looking out for us rather than just the pay cheque. Someone from outside the industry. Who knows how things could have worked out?'

'But things are better now, aren't they? You've continued to work and have a relationship with the Morpheme guys, or so I read.'

'Well, yeah. The last few years have been difficult for personal reasons. Like you said, life gets in the way and you wonder what you're doing or trying to do with it.'

'It's strange hearing you say that about life as if you experience a normal life like the rest of us mortals. I never thought of it that way before. I never thought of you and Morpheme in that way, as ordinary people.'

'You must realise there is the ideality of the band life and then there is real life. People make an awful lot of assumptions about a band.'

'That depends,' said Aurora and thought for a moment.
'On what?'

'Because I knew The Forum before they were famous, if you like, so they are real people to me. When I see interviews with them or read articles about them written by other journalists, I don't recognise them as the same band. I don't know that it's about assumptions, but rather perception.'

'OK, so you can see it from the band's point of view then?'

'In a way. But not with Morpheme, not with you, because I only ever knew you as a performing band that had a really big impact on my life. I see you as "the band", the "ideality", as you put it.'

'What kind of impact did we have on you? I'm always curious when people talk about Morpheme as life-changing or having an impact on fans and the music.'

Aurora looked down at her empty plate. When had she eaten her meal? Put on the spot. How honest should she be? How honest *could* she be with Oliver?

'First, it was, and still is your music that draws me to you. It's unlike anything else I've ever heard before, so different, it's hard to categorise and I love that. I can't say I was one of those teens who had issues at home. My parents are great, my life was good, I had no angst except the usual hormonal changes growing up. But, some of my friends did have problems at home and your music gave us a shared experience. I think back then your music was so different to everything else that was out there, and that is what attracted our group to you. We felt different to the others at college and the music reflected that difference and uncertainty of growing up in a world not of our making. I guess every generation feels that as they emerge into the existing world. Then, when I saw you perform at Hammersmith… wow! It's really difficult to find the words to explain the feeling of awe. It was almost like an out-of-body experience. I'm standing there in a crowd of mainly boys and men, fighting to keep my space, and then you come onto the stage, the music begins and I'm transported out of my body. All I am aware of is you guys on stage and the music thundering through me. I no longer feel aches in my back from standing around for hours; I no longer feel the elbows and knees of the people around me; I no longer have any bodily cravings or needs. All I feel is being there with you on the stage. The music and your performance are like a whirlpool sucking me in, and I lose all sense of myself. I lost all sense of my friends. That is an amazing experience and even though you are unaware of it, it feels like a shared experience. Whenever I listened to the music after that concert, it brought back a little piece of that sensation. A pleasure that I could replay whenever I was down or things weren't great in my life. In addition to that, whenever you brought out a new album, it was like a first date, getting to know you all over again and the musical surprises just kept coming. I don't think any other band has done that—for me at least.'

Too honest by far.

'I've never heard anyone analyse their experience in that way before!'

'You must have been to a concert, seen a performance that made you feel that way?'

'Well, yeah, but I don't recognise that kind of experience. But, then again, the bands were just OK. We went for something to do, rather than because we really liked the music.'

'I can't understand how someone who creates such amazing music that is so diverse in influences and tastes, doesn't feel some kind of connection to the music they listen to?'

'Ah, now, that's different. If I hear something I really like or that affects me, then yeah, I guess there is a connection there. I can't say I've lost myself completely though.'

'You should try it!' smiled Aurora. What was she doing?

'Wow, I never thought I'd be having a conversation like this with a fan.'

'Not the usual fan meeting you're used to, especially after yesterday.'

'No. Not the first time fans have fainted or had a nosebleed, but then those things tend to happen at concerts, not in a quiet gallery. I apologise. I thought I'd scared you. People have told me I can be an ass sometimes and I suppose if you see those videos on YouTube, I do come across like that. But that was not my intention at all yesterday. I was just curious as to why that particular painting captured your attention.'

'Are you *really* interested?' asked Aurora.

'Yeah.'

'The painting is really complex. It doesn't speak to you like a landscape or portrait; it goes beyond that. It's a real Freudian mélange of life, death and sex. And there are so many parts that are separate, but also part of the whole, that it demands your complete attention. I love the use of colour as well, almost wisps of soft colour in contrast to the sharp scratches dividing the canvas. Another reason it gripped me so much was because it reminded me of my dreams—strange, frightening dreams.'

Oliver sat leaning forward, his chin placed on his right hand, absorbing Aurora's words.

'What are your dreams about, or is that too personal a question?'

'No, not personal, in that I don't understand why these dreams started at a time in my life when change was just round the corner, but I didn't know it at the time. The dreams were about you and Morpheme on stage. The impressions were from when I first saw you when I was 17, but there was a lot of darkness and pain associated with those dreams. Only, when you appeared, I felt safe. That was it really, more of a closing-in feeling and emotional stress, but I felt I could identify these feelings in the Matta painting. Does that make sense?'

'It does make sense. The surrealists were great innovators and I really enjoyed the exhibition, but it is strange that of all the dreams you had it was those of Morpheme that you linked to the painting. Did you feel that way about any of the other paintings or exhibits?'

'No, I can't say I had the same connection with the rest of the exhibition, and certainly you appearing out of nowhere made that connection even stronger.'

'I understand now, I mean, about your reaction.' Oliver shook his head. 'That must have been really strange yesterday.'

'What pulls *you* to the surrealists?' asked Aurora.

The waitress came to clear the table.

Oliver thought for a moment. He picked up his glass and then put it down, realising it was empty.

The waitress returned with the dessert menu. They ordered tea and coffee with lemon cheesecake.

'I think it's the composition of the paintings. You know, in some paintings it is more identifiable in terms of humans, animals, objects, even when they are placed in unusual positions and circumstances. But it's how the artist has brought those elements together to communicate their ideas. It's very much like writing a song. There are the musical elements, the lyrics, sounds, and messaging sometimes. I don't always want to make a song obvious in what it's saying. I want people to feel something. I hope that when people listen to my music, it engages them and brings about an emotional response. What that response is doesn't matter; it's personal. That was why you fascinated me yesterday. I really wanted to know what you were thinking, feeling, finding in that painting.'

Coffee, tea and dessert arrived.

'Well, now you know. I bet you didn't expect my response to include you though?' Aurora smiled, adding a slice of fresh lemon to her Darjeeling tea.

'I didn't expect this at all when I called out to you. It's a new experience for me.'

'What do you mean by "a new experience"?'

'You know, it's difficult to just meet people. I'm always "meeting" people through work, through my network, but not in such a random way.'

'Well, that's how most of us mortals meet each other, you know. Most relationships aren't random; they're through similar networks. But do you mean that it's difficult to meet different people, those not in the industry?'

'Um, yeah, I think you put it better than I did.'

'It was a new experience for me too. I don't usually faint with a nosebleed when I meet people.' She smiled and ate a piece of cheesecake. 'So, can I ask you about fans? Not specific fans, just generally?'

'What about them?' replied Oliver picking up his coffee cup and holding it in front of his face.

'How do you deal with them clamouring for your attention?'

'That is difficult. You know we spoke about the ideality of the band and the performer? But some fans don't understand that. It's like when people think an actor is the character they portray. They can't distinguish between reality and fiction. With a band there is a level of intimacy at a concert. You expressed that earlier. When Morpheme first started out, I really wanted to get the audience involved and get into the audience. But it became dangerous. You think you can control the crowd, but you can't. Everyone responds to the music differently. You want that reaction, but not when some fans start taking it out on others in the crowd, or on you. When we played the bigger venues, it was different. You have a lot of security. There is usually a different mix of people in the crowd, but the sheer number of people out there who come to see you... breathtaking. They've paid good money, stood around for hours on end, sometimes in the rain, in awful conditions just to see you. And the excitement and high you get from that is immense. You can feel the power you have when you're on stage and you want to give the crowd what they came for. The excitement and tension escalate as you push yourself to please the crowd and the crowd pushes back, wanting more, shouting louder. Sometimes it feels more like a war than a concert. Both sides pushing each other. But even within those massive crowds, you get the fans who feel they have a connection with you and project all their wants and desires onto you. It's impossible. How can you have a connection with someone who you might look at for a second as you scour the audience performing? And while I feel I have some responsibility to fans to autograph books and take photos, it doesn't extend to a relationship. Fans don't want you to have your privacy or a private life they don't know about.

'You know, I read a blog a couple of years ago that was linked to Morpheme content. It was about what a jerk I was. Apparently, this blogger was a Morpheme fan. She just went into this tirade about me. She didn't feel I appreciated "my fans" and felt I didn't give them the same time and respect as other performers. Usually, I don't care about the stuff that gets written about me, especially now—everyone is an online columnist with opinions—but this blog really pissed me off.'

'I think I know the blog you mean. I read it too. Don't worry, I thought it unfair and completely subjective. She obviously has a crush on you and feels slighted.'

'Yeah, but it's out there, isn't it? And if I engage to defend myself, which is my right, I get more abuse about fan-bashing. Why do fans think they have rights over you? The exchange has been made when they pay for the music. If you don't like the music, don't buy it. If you don't like the performance, don't go to the concert, but don't expect some deep connection, because there isn't any.'

'So, you want your fans to engage with your music and not with you?'

'You make me sound like a shitty old man.'

'What I mean is, you want any connection to be just about the music?'

'Not even a connection—a reaction to the music. Like your rection to the Matta painting. Just because you feel you have a reaction to the painting, you're not suddenly in love with Matta the man and hunting him down.'

'That would be difficult with him being dead,' smiled Aurora.

Oliver sighed and smiled.

'Don't you get what I'm saying?'

'I do. I'm sorry I asked the question now, but you did an excellent job of not answering my question directly.'

'I don't mind the autographs, the promotional tours and photos with fans. You just have to be patient. That I understand. It's part of the job, my responsibility to acknowledge the fans at that moment, in that space and time—you know, there are other distractions—then they get a photo with you, and your signature, and they walk away happy. That works for me. But it's the other fans, like that blogger, who want so much more. The connection that isn't there. And to be honest, that scares the shit out of me.'

'Do *I* scare you?' asked Aurora looking straight at Oliver, her lips turned up into an enigmatic smile.

Oliver smiled despite himself, looked down into his empty coffee cup and said, 'You're not a fan in my book. No, you don't scare me.' Then he looked up and added, 'You fascinate me.'

Aurora looked away. The command and calm she had experienced in the last 30 minutes of their dinner crashed and clattered like smashed plates. Her heart beat faster, her throat and mouth dried up and she tried to drink some tea, but the cup was empty.

'Why?' she whispered, unable to look at him.

'Aurora, look at me.'

Aurora looked up at him. She focused on his mouth so she wouldn't have to look into those amazing blue eyes.

'I find you fascinating because you're real to me. You are a person unconnected to my life, but through a love of art we came together. You're someone I want to know better; someone I feel close to. I really want to see you again.' There was an urgency in his voice, a pleading.

Aurora saw Oliver's lips move but couldn't comprehend the words he was speaking. She only noted the sound of his voice, a quivering, faltering bass voice.

'Can we order another drink?' she said suddenly, looking around frantically for the waitress.

Oliver sat back in his seat, confused by the dismissal. Why did she continually push him away?

The waitress appeared.

'Can I have another bottle of water please?' asked Aurora.

'Sir?'

'A glass of Vino Santo,' sighed Oliver.

The waitress cleared away the cluttered dishes and used napkins, exposing the white tablecloth, bare and pale with smudges here and there.

Oliver and Aurora sat in silence, waiting for their drinks. The happy chatter of people at other tables filled the void. Aurora tried not to think. She couldn't speak and desperately needed to drink something as her throat burned. She felt herself fall into the sweat and stress of her entrance. Oh God, why had she agreed to this dinner? Because she wanted more than anything to be close to Oliver, to be near him, touching him, wanting him. But he was like a Greek statue to her, so close to touch, but she dared not in case she damaged him in some way. How could she get beyond that? How could she bring him down from that podium she'd placed him on?

The drinks arrived.

Aurora gulped down her water, bubbles and all. She hiccupped. Oliver allowed himself a small smile.

Aurora's mind was still racing. She needed to say something not to leave this awkward silence. Oliver was still looking at her, watching her as she drank, hiding behind the glass. She stood up and excused herself, running to the bathroom. Shutting the door of the cubicle, she sat down and held her crying head in her hands. This was the man she had fantasised over, wanted to be close to, and wanted to know better. She had been ready to give herself over to him at any point had he asked. So what was she doing sitting in the toilet trying to work out an answer to his request to see her again? He was asking her! Oliver, lead singer of Morpheme! She wiped her eyes and relieved herself. Walking out to wash her hands, she saw her puffy red face in the mirror. And yet her face did not reflect the confused horror she felt inside. Why did she feel like this? She couldn't understand it. She had to say yes to his request to see her. She knew she would regret the alternative. Aurora dried her hands and face, reapplied her minimal make-up and repeated the word 'yes' to herself five times. She walked back to her table and sat down.

Desire

They left the restaurant to walk around The Green, a small open park with a fish pond, shrubs and flowers. It was a calming contrast to the noise and bustle of the warm restaurant and Aurora was already feeling more in control. She planned to walk around for a few minutes and then make her excuse to go home. Although it was dark and chilly, the lights surrounding The Green offered an electric moonlight.

Oliver walked close to her. She felt he wanted to get closer but was hesitant. She knew what he wanted, but what did she want? Oliver was no longer the phantasmagoria he had once been. This was real and she had to make a real decision that would impact on both their lives. Did she really want to know the man walking beside her? Yes. On a personal level as well as a professional level. Did she want a physical relationship with this man? Wasn't that the fantasy? The draw on stage, the sex appeal of the famous? But what a shallow feeling that was. What would she have done if Oliver had asked her out when she was 17? She thought she would give herself without hesitation, but would she really? Couldn't that situation have morphed into something less fantastic and more horror-based? Now she was nearing fifty, he was a few years older and they had both experienced abortive relationships. After David, Aurora felt she didn't need that type of relationship, so why did she experience the reactions she had with Oliver? Why did she feel like she was 17 again: excited, nervous, unable to respond.

'Shall we sit down?' asked Oliver.

Aurora flew back to the moment and sat down without saying anything.

'Are you cold?' Oliver asked Aurora, moving closer to her.

'I'm fine, thank you,' she replied. Why was she lying?

She looked up at the lights. The ice-blue white hurt her eyes, but she continued to stare and think. Wasn't she just sabotaging herself again? Here was an opportunity unlike any she had known before, waiting for her, but all she could do was ignore him. She remembered what Jennie had said to her. Jennie's face came into her mind, telling her off. Aurora took a deep breath and made a decision.

'What did you mean when you said you wanted to see me again?'

'Um, well, you know, to meet up with you, over dinner, or lunch, or at a gallery. Like a date, but...'

Aurora looked up at Oliver.

'Yes?'

'But if you don't want to, just say so and I won't contact you again,' he replied, despondent.

'I do want to see you, but you've got to understand what this is like for me. I'm really nervous and in awe of you.

You were my fantasy and now you're asking me out. I'm finding this difficult to reconcile.'

'Don't think of me in that way. I'm just an old guy now, but I know now more than ever what it is I want from a relationship and it's you.'

'But you don't know me,' said Aurora looking at Oliver.

'I know enough from yesterday that you are someone I want to get to know better. You know, your reaction is part of that attraction for me. You push me away and I've not had that before. People may hate me and throw things at me, but they always do what I say. You're so different from everyone else I know.'

Aurora could see the logic behind Oliver's argument. She stood up from the bench and walked towards the pond. Oliver waited, unsure of what he should say or do next.

Aurora turned to face Oliver. He stood up, looking at her hopefully. Damn it, why did she have such a hook in him?

'OK, let's give it a try,' she said smiling and finally relaxing. Oliver rushed over to her and took her hand in his, squeezing her fingers as he looked into Aurora's green eyes. He brought her hands up to his mouth and kissed them. Aurora giggled. Suddenly everything had changed. Aurora had made a decision. All her anxieties and stresses had left her the moment she'd agreed to see him. Aurora was so close to Oliver. She could really see his face now, the harsh white glare exposing his age. And yet in his jaw-line, in his mouth, his electric blue eyes, she saw the man who had haunted her dreams for so long. She felt as if she was falling in love with him again. Only now it was real.

Aurora lowered her hands and put them around Oliver's waist, under his jacket. His slim physique, hard, solid and oh, how warm he felt. Oliver, in return, circled his arms around Aurora's waist, pressing her closer to him (as if that were possible). He felt her breath on his neck and closed his eyes. Oh, how he needed this woman. She was all at once a mature woman and a girl, unsure of herself, yet she knew what she wanted. It had been years since he'd felt so excited by another person. He leaned his head down, kissed Aurora's neck, her throat, her chin and finally found her mouth: soft, supple, quivering. He kissed her softly and tenderly. It was the ending to their evening he'd wanted.

Aurora felt Oliver's body as if it were a part of her. Now in this proximity and with the decision behind her, an overpowering physical want and desire overtook her. She held him tight, leaning on his neck, gently kissing like whisps of soft petals against his skin. He moved his head and kissed her, finding her mouth again. Aurora ached for him. His gentleness and care inflamed her and she wanted to suck him all up. As his lips, his so soft lips, sought hers, she responded, gently, softly. Her hunger for him grew as she sought his tongue, sought his mouth, ever wider, wanting to climb into him.

They both trembled with pleasure and desire as Aurora let herself go, her body no longer held back by indecision and stress, having found what it needed, hands feeling Oliver's back, his stomach, his thighs.

Oliver, excited by Aurora's change, felt her body, felt her hands everywhere. Like a branding he could still feel the heat from her hands after she'd moved them. They kissed, mouths open wide, searching for each other.

Oliver wanted Aurora, but they would have to be patient. He withdrew. Painfully.

'You've made me very happy,' he said holding her hands.

Aurora hugged and held onto Oliver, now unwilling to let him go at all. She wanted everything from him now. That portal between ideality and reality was open and she had stepped through.

'I want you,' she whispered into his ear. 'I want you now. I want you to come back with me. Tonight,' she said, her face serious, her eyes wide, while her body seemed to move up and down as emotions raged. She was on fire as the blood rushed between her legs, pulsating, throbbing, aching. Her body now remembered what it was like to feel passion coursing through every part of her.

Oliver felt the changes in her body, his own body responding with blood rushes and a flooding of excitation.

He looked up, separating himself from Aurora. He took her hand in his and walked towards the train station. He ordered a taxi and they waited, together, in silence, still connected. The taxi ride was painful, strapped in separately; party music and a chatty driver blocked their bond.

But they continued to hold hands, fingers stroking, hand-holding warming.

Once through the door of Aurora's flat, she pulled Oliver into the bedroom. All her anxieties—David, the divorce, redundancy and her new career—floated away like mist on a lake. She knew what she wanted and now she was courageous enough to take it.

Closing the door behind them, Aurora pushed Oliver up against the door, stripping his jacket off, her jacket off, kissing him, tasting him, her tongue urging him to follow her lead.

He followed, feeling she had let herself go straight into his trust, his life. The Matta painting came back to him as they touched, ached, felt, groped in the dark, seeking more than their bodies, hungry for what each of them brought to this union.

Oliver's hands reached for Aurora's skirt. He fumbled, the zip gave way and it sank past her hips, freeing her body from its restraint. He sought her legs and felt tights. A barrier to be overcome. Aurora stepped back a moment and removed them and, within a second, she was on top of Oliver, pushing him hard against the door. Her passion and strength overwhelmed him and he stripped her shirt off, pushing her towards the bed. Even in the dark, they felt instinctively where the other was. Their space opened up, moulding around them, enveloping them in an armour of palpability. Oliver's hands explored Aurora's body. He wanted to touch every part of her, wanted to energise her, bring her to a point of perturbed passion. Every touch was heightened by their life experiences. No one else could understand their needs: only they could satiate each other's appetites, forced and provoked by years of disappointments.

Aurora gasped as Oliver's hands found the inside of her legs, his arms strong and yet his hands eager and soft, stroking her, feeling her, responding to her every ripple. Aurora found Oliver's trouser zip, undoing it and freeing him from his trousers. She felt his penis, hard and eager in anticipation. She closed her eyes as she held him gently. A wave of white flashing fell from her head through her body down into her vagina, filling her up. She was ready to burst in her passion as she reached the pleasurable ache of her female hard-on.

Oliver withdrew for a moment. Aurora heard searching in pockets and then a tearing sound. She removed her bra and knickers and moved onto the bed, pushing the duvet away. She lay waiting, her hands warm, stroking herself, sustaining her excitement such that it was enough to remain just on edge. She felt Oliver touch her leg, feel his way up her body, kissing, stroking, licking her hand, which was still stroking and playing. Sliding upwards, his lips surprised her nipples as he sucked hard and fast, his passion escaping, pouring all over her. His lips found hers and they hungrily devoured each other as Oliver slipped into Aurora. They both gasped as each was flooded with sensations like a thousand bubbles bursting on skin. Aurora lost herself in a blur of colours: blues and green turning purple and red. And then as she thrust and parried with Oliver, the orgasm shot through her body like an earthquake tremor. She felt as if she was in another space and time, beyond the bedroom, London, the planet. She had never felt this before, and gasping to breathe, she held onto Oliver, afraid to let him go in case she fell back down to earth, to reality.

Oliver could no longer feel Aurora. She was a part of him, subsumed into his every movement. They crashed into each other, bringing such a climax that Oliver felt he was in an ethereal dreamscape. Aurora's body, in a trembling seizure, increased his climax several times.

And then there was calm.

They were both exhausted, emotionally and physically. Oliver kissed Aurora on her forehead, cheek and mouth as he moved to separate from her body, not *her*, only her body.

Aurora revived and slowly returned to herself. She lay in the dark, listening to Oliver moving about before he climbed back onto her. They were both sweating, exuding parfum de sex and it smelt wonderful. Oliver took Aurora in his arms. Neither of them wanted to say anything, avoiding any shattering of the attractive universe their bodies had created.

Finally, in the warm lull of their bodies, they fell asleep.

*

Aurora woke with a start. She shivered. Then, reaching for the duvet, she felt the weight of Oliver's arm across her waist. Still in the darkness, reality had not pierced the bubbles of the previous night. But she had to get up. Other physical needs had to be met. She gently moved Oliver's arm and while she felt around for her underwear in the modulating dark of early morning, he turned onto his front and slept.

After relieving herself and a quick douche and mouthwash, she went into the kitchen for a glass of water. With a second glass for herself, she poured another and took it for Oliver, who was still sleeping. But Aurora was wide awake. And thinking.

After some time, Oliver woke up. Having slept heavily, he felt groggy and full of the night's warmth. Recalling the whole evening, he slipped into a gratified stupor but then noticed Aurora sitting in a chair in the corner of the room, reading. Rubbing his eyes, he forced himself awake. Had he overstayed his welcome? He sat up in the bed, pulling the duvet to his waist.

'Good morning,' he said softly.

'Good morning,' replied Aurora smiling. 'There's a glass of water for you,' she said, pointing to his right.

As he drank the water, Aurora returned to the bed, kneeling on the edge, like a young girl, unsure of her next move.

'Don't go away, I'll be back in a minute,' said Oliver smiling with his blue eyes. And how blue they looked now. An intense electric blue as they flashed in that smile.

Aurora sat on the bed, let her legs dangle off the side like a child. Maybe Oliver would help her restart her life, if she would let him.

'Come here,' said Oliver returning to the bed after freshening up. Pulling Aurora to him, he hugged and kissed her, the tingling sensations of the night returning, exciting them both.

They lay together for a short time, quietly, calmly, warmly, taking in each other's dimensions. Aurora thought about how they had met, the circumstances that had led up to this most amazing moment of her life. Here she was lying in the arms of a man she had fantasised about for years. A man she thought she would do anything for and be grateful for the privilege of just being close to him. She didn't feel she could ask anything of him just yet. Her expectations of this burgeoning relationship were low.

She wanted to see what his reaction would be, what his relationship requirements were. Oliver stroked her face, gently pushing back her hair. She closed her eyes, heightening the feel of his soft and gentle fingers. She breathed in to feel the moment. Why couldn't they stay like this forever? Just lying together, no talking, no sound except for their breathing. She felt calmer now and she wanted to remain in this calm state. Aurora envisioned a portrait, just a face and a gentle hand. The longing, the soft love and promise of a moment. She saw it painted in oranges and yellows, portraying the warmth of the moment. She was glowing. She gave herself completely to Oliver.

*

'What are your plans for the next few days?' Oliver asked Aurora as they were enjoying a brunch of toast, mushroom pâté, tomatoes and watercress in Aurora's kitchen. They were seated by the window, the warm sun beaming on them both while they ate.

'I've got four interviews and three nights out at the bars and pubs. It doesn't sound like much, but the rest of my time is taken up in preparation. Why?' replied Aurora smiling and avoiding Oliver's look.

'You know why. Don't turn those amazing green eyes away from me,' he smiled, stretching his arm out to lift Aurora's chin so he could look into them.

'You make me feel like a teenager, I don't know how I'm supposed to act. It's been such a long time since I've been with anyone,' replied Aurora.

'You have the same effect on me. I don't know what I'm supposed to do, but I do know I want to see you again and I want to be near you. Whatever that looks like for us I don't know, but we have to be together.'

'I want to be with you as well, Oliver. I guess we'll have to work it out. As to my next few days, I have to work, but why don't you join me this evening? I'm going to the Dog and Duck tonight. There's a decent line-up. I'd be interested in your take on the bands and the music.'

'You're on. Shall I meet you here?'

'Meet me at the pub by five. I'll grab a table. If you come here, I know we'll end up being late,' said Aurora smiling at Oliver.

'You're right, better not give in to the temptation,' he said winking at her.

As Oliver was dressing, Aurora checked her mobile for messages. A message from Jennie and two missed calls. David's number.

'I'd better get moving if I'm going to make it back in time.'

Aurora grabbed Oliver and hugged him as if she wouldn't let him go. He was surprised but relieved that she felt the same way about him. He held her tight for a minute, and she eased her hold enough to look up at him. He kissed her softly, all his emotions translating into that gentle exchange. Aurora's chest constricted as she closed her eyes and let herself go. All at once there was terror and love as she held onto Oliver, not wanting to let him go. He kissed her forehead and hugged her again. She knew this was where she would have to let him go, release him to see him again. She let go, struggling to pull her arms away from him. As he opened the door to leave, he turned back, took her hand in his and kissed her palm and fingers.

'I'll see you in a few hours,' he said. And then he was gone. Aurora shut the door and fell to the floor crying.

*

Aurora had to get some fresh air. She showered, changed into some jeans and an orange blouse and left her flat. As she walked out of her building, she noticed a parked car across the road. A man was sitting behind the wheel. It was David. Aurora froze. David got out of his car as he realised he had been seen. He was trying too hard to make this look like a casual meeting. Aurora started walking towards the High Street. She didn't want to engage with him.

'Aurora, wait.' That voice still filled her with dread.

She heard him come up behind her when suddenly he grabbed her arm. She turned on him and pushed him away.

'I don't want to talk to you, David.'

'Why not? I only want a little bit of your time. Is that too much to ask from a wife?'

'Ex-wife. Why won't you just leave me alone? I told you I would call the police if you contacted me again. And why are you parked outside my flat?'

'I can park wherever I want. So, who's the guy?'

'What guy?'

'The guy I saw leaving about an hour ago.'

'Why do you assume he's with me?'

'I saw you together last night.'

'Oh my God! You are actually spying on me!'

'I'm protecting you. I only have your best interests at heart, Aurora,' said David softly, reaching to touch her face. Aurora turned away from him abruptly as if he had scorched her.

'You've never had my interests at heart. It was only ever what *you* wanted. And don't touch me. This is getting beyond a joke, David. Why can't you just move on, meet someone else? Leave me alone.'

'There isn't anyone like you Aurora. Look, I know not everything was perfect, but it wasn't that bad, surely? I want you back.'

'You have a very selective memory. Nineteen years! And in that time, you constantly promised to change, but you didn't. You don't own me, David, and you can't control my life anymore,' said Aurora, her voice trembling as she recalled the years of David's treatment. She had to get away from him. She hurried to the High Street.

David continued to follow her. This was harassment, but how could she prove it? She was almost at the High Street. She was rushing, trying to keep away from David and trying to be seen by others. She looked around at the shops. What was going to be her safest option? She went into the pharmacy; they knew her there and she could get help if she needed it. She entered and walked up to the perfumes near the counter. She turned to look behind her. She thought she was safe and David had left her, but then she saw him standing outside the pharmacy. What could she do?

'Hi Aurora. How are you?'

She turned to see Lesley, the pharmacy manager standing next to her smiling.

'Oh, Lesley, it's good to see you. I'm fine, but I need a favour. Is there any way that you can let me leave the pharmacy by the back door?'

Lesley's smile dropped.

'Are you OK?'

'My ex-husband is waiting outside. Can you see him, just by the window? He's trying not to be seen.'

'Yes, I see him. Is he harassing you? Shall I call the police?'

'No, it's OK, I just want to get home, but I don't want to face him. I wouldn't ask, but—'

'Come with me.' And she took Aurora's hand, checking first to see if David was watching them by the window. As soon as he moved back from the window, she pulled Aurora behind the counter and into the back office.

'Now, listen, are you sure you don't want me to call the police? What do you think he will do when he discovers you've left here?'

'No, don't call the police. I will sort it out. I just need some time.'

'I don't like this. You're shaking. Let me walk you home.'

'Oh no, Lesley, really, you've got to work. I'm OK. Really.'

'No, you're not. Besides, it's slow today. Dan and Bridget can handle the shop for a short time. I'm not taking no for an answer. Wait here a second. Wait!' said Lesley, reinforcing her command with her look at Aurora.

Lesley disappeared, leaving Aurora alone. What was she going to do about David? She couldn't let him affect her life like this. What would he do if he was sure she was seeing Oliver? He had been crazy enough when they were married. If he felt he didn't have anything to lose…

Lesley reappeared.

'All good. Come on. Your ex is still standing around outside. He keeps looking in. I've asked Dan to speak to him in a couple of minutes.'

They walked out of the back office, into the tight corridor, past the kitchen and consulting rooms and out into a courtyard. There were potted plants and bushes dotted around and a bistro table and chairs. It was nicely done. To the side there was a wooden gate the height of the wall, and this is where Lesley and Aurora exited onto a quiet back street. Lesley led Aurora further away from the High Street. She had never been in this part of town and was disorientated. That shifting feeling again.

'You don't need to tell me, but it may help to talk,' suggested Lesley.

'Lesley, I'm really grateful for your help. I do owe you some explanation at least. I divorced David two years ago. I thought everything was fine, he would move on. But he continues calling me and sending me flowers. I've told him I'm not interested and I will call the police, but he just keeps coming back. I don't even know how he got my new address!'

'Aurora, you need to report this behaviour.'

'I'm just afraid of what he's capable of. I was married to this man for 19 years. We separated for a short time, but he convinced me that he really loved me, that he wasn't "that" man and that he needed me. I resisted for months, but the pull was too strong. I don't know if it was him convincing me or me not wanting to be alone after a failed marriage. Somewhere in my head I was certain it was the former.'

'Can I be honest with you, Aurora?'

'Yes.'

'We don't know each other well, but I do know this situation well. My sister went through an abusive marriage. I know you think that is not what your marriage was, but believe me, words are really powerful and you need to call this out for what it is: an abusive relationship. No one has rights over another human being. Please promise me you will speak to the police about this. I don't want to see you in hospital like my sister. And that was a close call, believe me.'

Lesley stopped at a junction.

'Where do you live?'

'B— Avenue. I think we may need to walk back a bit.'

'I know where that is. We're OK. It's best if we turn left here and we can walk up through the park, which takes us near the railway line and then the back of B— Avenue.'

'How do you know your way around this area so well?' asked Aurora.

'Medicine deliveries and visits. I try and cycle when I can, so I can take short cuts that the cars can't take.'

'Ah, I should have realised. I just assumed you used couriers.'

'We could, but it would be expensive and also we get to know our customers better that way. They like the personal service. But anyway, I'm more concerned about you and your current situation.'

Lesley's phone pinged.

'Dan says David made a scene but left abruptly when he realised you weren't there. Come on, we have to hurry. It should only take another ten minutes if we walk quickly.'

They were almost running as they exited the park and Lesley led Aurora through a short cut, over the railway bridge, through another short cut between houses and gardens and then suddenly they were on B— Avenue.

'This way,' said Aurora as they rushed towards her block of flats. David's car was still parked across the road. Aurora stopped and took a photo of the car and registration number.

'Thank you, Lesley, I'll be OK now,' said Aurora. 'I don't want you getting involved unnecessarily.'

'It *is* necessary. You get indoors and don't let him into your flat. Can I call you later? I have your number on our system.'

'Please do,' said Aurora as she hugged Lesley.

'Thank you.'

'Get indoors.' Then Lesley left.

Aurora climbed up the stairs, her legs aching from the tense and hurried walk home. And then she was in her flat.

She locked the door, closed the curtains, remaining in the dark, too sacred to switch the lights on. She needed to do something. Only a couple more hours before she left for the Dog and Duck.

The quiet of the encroaching evening was broken by a car engine revving and then the car speeding away. Aurora went over to the lounge window and carefully moved the curtain, just allowing her a glimpse of David's car. Then it was gone. She sighed, deeply relieved that the episode had passed. She made herself a cup of tea and then stood in the darkening lounge for a few minutes, her eyes closed, wishing that everything would stop.

Her phone pinged. Was it David? She didn't care. He was *not* going to continue controlling her. She picked up her phone. A message from Oliver:

Can't wait to see you – missing you. Xx

Despite everything, the message brought a smile to her face. She finished her tea then messaged him back:

Missing you more than you know. Xx

She changed into grey trousers, a black tank top and her favourite grey jacket, grabbed her work bag and left her flat, hoping David wasn't waiting for her on another road.

*

Aurora walked into the Dog and Duck, which was busier than she expected it to be at this time. She looked around but couldn't see Oliver. She felt relieved that she would have time to get a drink and a table. She walked over to the bar and said hi to Nigel. She ordered a tonic water and a brandy. The brandy tasted strong to her, but its warmth spread through her body, reclaiming her resilience. She left the empty glass at the bar and took her tonic water to her favourite spot where she went through her preparation tasks when her phone rang. She didn't recognise the number.

'Hello?'

'Hi Aurora. It's Lesley. How are you?'

'I'm fine. Thank you for walking me home today. I really appreciate what you did.'

'Have you spoken to the police?'

'Not yet, but I promise I will. I had to get ready for work so didn't have the time. But I will.'

'Please, Aurora, don't wait. Do it as soon as possible. I don't want to see you hurt.'

'I will. I'll do it tomorrow. I promise I'll call the police first thing. I have to go now. Thanks. Bye.'

'What's happened?' asked Oliver as he sat down next to Aurora.

'Oh, nothing. I just needed to check on something that's all. Hi.'

'Hi,' said Oliver as he leaned in to kiss Aurora. She leaned in too but gave him her cheek, blushing in the public space.

'How was your afternoon?'

'Oh, quiet. I just went for a walk.'

'What are you drinking? Would you like another?'

'Yes please. Just tonic water, the Fever-Tree Indian Tonic water.'

Oliver made his way to the bar, giving Aurora some time to consider Lesley's call. She understood Lesley was concerned for her and even though she had threatened David with the police herself, actually speaking to them and potentially making a formal complaint against him was something completely different. It scared her. It would take her down a path that would consume her life. She had had enough of David and his games. The divorce had been painful and protracted and he had used every option available to him to delay, obstruct and deny her closure. What were her options realistically? Wouldn't it be easier to move away? He would soon give up, wouldn't he? But then he would harass her parents in the same way he had done when they had separated and she had left him and got the divorce under way. She wished he would just disappear. Her head began to ache. She wanted to go home.

'What are you thinking about?' asked Oliver, placing the drinks on the table.

Aurora looked up surprised, smiled unconvincingly and drank her tonic water.

'Just about work,' she lied.

'You looked like you were really concentrating. I didn't mean to disturb you.'

'No, it's fine. Let's enjoy this evening.'

Oliver smiled. As he shifted his chair to get a better view of the stage and sit closer to Aurora, he turned his head slightly to look at her. She seemed distracted, concerned about something. He put his arm around her shoulder and squeezed. The more she seemed to pull back, the more he wanted her. He wanted to protect her, be there for her. Now that she was a part of his life, he couldn't imagine life without her and his passion for her grew the more conflicted she seemed. She was everything that he needed in his life.

The live music started and it was time for Aurora to work.

The first two bands were OK. Aurora scribbled away, finding positives in their music and performance. Oliver watched Aurora. He had never seen anyone take so much care and consideration for their work before, particularly when there was so much pressure to conform to the newest music trends. He was fascinated when she closed her eyes, really listening to the music and giving her full attention to the performance. No wonder she was in demand. She was a musician's dream.

That was when it occurred to him that Aurora was the one to help him with his comeback. With her integrity in the music business and increasing interest in band biographies, working with her would be an opportunity he couldn't afford to ignore. All kinds of scenes played in Oliver's mind as he allowed himself a glimpse at a potential future of award-winning albums and mega-concerts. Could he convince Morpheme to regroup for a world tour? If he couldn't, he knew their number one fan could. The guys would buy into anything Aurora said. They would listen to someone like her.

There was a break before the next band came on and Aurora went to the bathroom. Oliver watched the set change. A nostalgic feeling came over him as he recalled his own early days in Morpheme. The places they had played were complete dregs: smoke-filled, back alleyway places. Dark and dangerous. In those days, they had had no fear. They just did what they needed to do to achieve their goal. It had been over five years since he had last performed live. Despite not having the same energy as he had in the past, he loved live performance. The energy of the audience could drive you to do anything.

'Oh my God! Are you Oliver from Morpheme?' an excited man in his forties —beard, leather jacket—asked Oliver.

'Excuse me?' replied Oliver.

'You are, aren't you? I can't believe this. Could I get a photo with you?'

'Um, yeah, OK. I'm surprised you recognised me. What's your name?'

'Brian. Thanks. I would recognise you anywhere,' he said as he shook Oliver's hand, hauled him up, put his arm around his waist and took a photo of them both together. This attention did not go unnoticed and soon there were a number of people requesting photos and autographs.

Just as Nigel arrived to see what was going on, Aurora also returned to find Oliver surrounded by a mini-mob of fans. She smiled. Oliver seemed in his element. Did he miss this, she wondered? Nigel came up to her.

'Who is he?' he asked.

'Oliver Coslett from Morpheme,' replied Aurora laughing as Oliver had another photo taken.

'Seriously?'

'Yes, seriously.'

'Aurora, why didn't you tell me? I could have arranged something.'

'He was just joining me for a drink. He wasn't expecting this, but I think he likes the attention,' she said smiling.

'Should I do anything?'

'No, look they've calmed down now and the next band are due to start.'

'Let me bring you some drinks at least?'

'OK. Can I have a black tea?' Then she made her way past the last few fans and turned to Oliver saying, 'Oliver, this is Nigel. He's the pub manager. Nigel, this is Oliver.'

'It's great to meet you,' Nigel said. 'I was telling Aurora if I had known you were coming, I could have done something.'

'Hi Nigel. Well, this was unplanned really, but thanks.'

'Would you like another drink?'

'Uh, yeah, thanks. I'll have another Pilsner.'

'Thanks, Nigel. The next band is starting their set,' Aurora said turning to her notepad. Had this been a bad idea?

Nigel returned to the bar to get their order. This was great. Would Aurora write about Oliver being at the pub as well? He would have to check with her, convince her that this was a great opportunity for everyone concerned.

They returned their attention to the stage and the next band.

After the fourth band, Nigel brought over their drinks. Aurora was grateful for the tea. The effect of the brandy had worn off some time ago and while her main concern was her work and Oliver, David's insidious effect lingered within her.

'Aurora, will you write about Oliver being here tonight?' asked Nigel.

'Well, I wasn't going to,' she said, then turning to him asked, 'Oliver, how would you feel about it?'

'Why not? You might as well. It might be all over social media anyway.'

'I hadn't thought about that,' said Nigel.

'OK, I'll mention something, but I don't want to take anything away from the bands.'

'Thanks. This kind of publicity is great.' And Nigel left with all sorts of exciting thoughts racing through his head.

Aurora was unsure.

'I'm happy for you to write about me, but you don't seem enthusiastic about it?' Oliver said.

'I like doing these venues because it gives new bands a chance to be noticed. If I include you in the article, it's going to completely detract from the bands playing here tonight.'

'I wish we'd had someone like you looking out for *us* when we were starting out. Why don't you write a separate piece? I'd love to be interviewed by you,' said Oliver beaming his smile at her.

'That could work. We could do the interview here. Let's discuss it another time.'

The final band came on, popular as 'Nigel's Pick'.

After the final performance, Aurora was ready to leave. She suddenly felt very fragile and wanted the security of her flat and recognisable things around her. She told Nigel she would be in touch about a separate article. He shook her hand gratefully. Oliver was still talking to people. She felt jealous, excluded. This was not her Oliver, it was the ideality, and she didn't like it. Because now she had the real him, she didn't want to share him. He was laughing and joking with people when he looked over to her. She tried to smile but felt exhausted. He said goodnight to his devotees and walked over to Aurora.

'Are you OK?'

'I'm just tired and I still need to write up my notes,' she said, excusing herself.

'Let's get you home.'

Aurora allowed herself to be taken home. After a hug and a kiss, Oliver left, promising to call her the following morning.

Aurora struggled to stay awake. She was exhausted and yet the fear that David was outside, watching, clawed

148

at her. Unable to stand it any longer, she looked out of the window. No car. She fell asleep relieved.

*

'How are you this morning?' asked Oliver. Aurora could hear a touch of excitement in his voice. His tone was different from what she was used to.

'OK, still a little tired, but OK.'

'I want to talk to you. Can I come over, or we can meet somewhere?'

'Come over. I'm not in the mood to go out and I've got a pile of work to get through,' she sighed.

'I'll be there in an hour.'

Aurora was still in bed, struggling to exert herself. But eventually, she clambered out, made a cup of tea, checked outside her window—this was now becoming a compulsion, damn him—and had a shower. No car. She felt better. Maybe it was over? A twinkle of cheerfulness lit her thoughts and she was almost happy when she came out of the bathroom. Then the buzzer rang.

'Hello Aurora,' said Oliver, reaching for her. He held her tight and kissed her on her forehead. How did he know that was what she needed? She held him tight. The feel and scent of him centred her, renewed her.

'I've brought some items,' he said, presenting a spray of yellow and orange carnations, gypsophilia and deep green fern leaves. Aurora couldn't help but smile.

'I've also brought some lunch. If you're happy for me to cook, I thought you could do some work while I prepare lunch, and then we can talk.'

'I'm impressed. What's for lunch?'

'Fresh tagliatelle with fresh tomatoes and basil, and orange sorbet for dessert. I wanted to keep lunch light. Do you approve?'

'Absolutely wonderful!'

Aurora followed Oliver into her kitchen and quickly showed him where everything was that he might need for cooking and serving. She poured herself a glass of water and left him to it.

Lunch was an epicurean affair, the pasta complemented beautifully with a glass of Primitivo wine.

'I didn't know you could cook.'

'I don't give away all my secrets to journalists.'

'My dad would be impressed.'

'Does he cook?'

'He used to have his own restaurants. He's retired now though, but still likes to cook for the family.'

'Are *you* impressed?'

'Definitely. The meal was wonderful. Thank you.'

Oliver served the orange sorbet.

'You know I'm crazy about you,' he started. Aurora froze. The 'but' was coming. She remained silent.

'But last night really brought back to me how much I miss being a performer and being part of something larger than me. Meeting those fans last night was great. I really didn't think I had missed it so much. You know, I actually thought I was done with it. But no, the energy, the excitement, the thrill of being with those people really got under my skin. I was still buzzing when I got home. I can't explain it, it was just so different to my past experiences. I don't know if it's because I'm older, or that the fans are older, but it felt great. You know, we briefly talked about doing an interview?'

Aurora nodded.

'Well, I still want to do the interview, but I want to make a few calls first. I want to start planning a tour. What do you think?' Oliver's eyes shone brightly, he was smiling and open-mouthed, waiting for Aurora's enthusiasm.

'You don't need my permission to do this, Oliver.'

'But I do want your support and your time. How would you feel about going on tour with me?'

Aurora gasped. She wasn't sure what to say. On the one hand, it would be amazing, exciting, thrilling to be with Oliver on tour. Spending time with him travelling, really getting to know him in all his moods. Then there was the work. She would have exclusive material and access to him. Her career would explode and she could get at least a book out of it. And then there was the possibility of leaving David behind. She could put her stuff into storage and rent her flat out. David would have no idea where she was. It all felt so positive, as if this was the answer to all of her problems. But there was the other side. How would she view Oliver after the tour? Seeing him close up, in his element, potentially under stress, reunited with the band? How would those dynamics work and where would that leave her? A black thought, like a large fly, buzzed around her head. *Is he using me?* She swatted it away, ashamed it had even come to her. Their meeting had been a random occurrence. But why did he want her along? And she wouldn't have time for her other work. No time for anything else except Oliver and the tour. Would her family and friends forgive her?

'Don't make up your mind now. I know it's a lot to take in and there is still a lot to plan out. I've been thinking things through. You know, meeting you has been such an amazing experience. I feel alive again, my energy has returned. And last night, well, I just can't stop thinking about it. I've almost finished the new album and the timing is just perfect.' Oliver was wide-eyed and leaning forward, almost touching Aurora. 'You haven't said anything.'

'Oliver, I'm flattered. Really, I am, but I do need some time to think about this. I'm worried a tour could jeopardise our relationship and I don't want that. Can you give me a couple of days?'

'No problem. Nothing is arranged yet. I do want you with me though. I can't see how that could affect our relationship, except to make it stronger. In the past, the issue was always that I was away, but if you come with me, we can be together and you can still work. I'll make sure you have exclusives to any interviews. As far as I see it, it's a win-win situation for both of us.'

'You're very confident of that.'

'I want you with me on this tour.'

'What if I decided I couldn't or didn't want to go?'

'It would depend on your reasons.'

'You want this tour so much?'

'Yes.'

'OK.'

'Okay, yes? You're coming?'

'Yes, OK. I'll go with you, but you need to give me time. I can't just drop everything.'

Oliver grabbed Aurora, kissing and hugging her, literally taking her breath away. She would have giggled had she been able to breathe. Oliver seemed like a child to her in that moment. She wondered about his reaction: his joy at getting his way and his taking her agreement as immediate. She worried that he had not considered the reality of such a huge undertaking; that the evening full of fan excitement and recognition, the live music and the atmosphere had triggered the adrenaline rush he had felt in the past. She felt he had not considered the reality of what would come with this renewed turn of fame. He was thinking of the ideality, *not* the reality.

For her, it was an opportunity to be with Oliver, to spend time with him, work with him, eat with him, travel with him, live him. She had no time to consider how such an immediate decision would affect their undeveloped relationship. She had no doubt it would benefit her career, but to her that wasn't the primary focus. She felt a fogginess float in, such that she couldn't see the danger she felt. For a moment, the danger made its presence felt and then disappeared in the fog. Aurora dismissed the feeling, dismissed her instinct, and the moment passed.

Oliver was so excited by it all, he cleared away the dishes and wanted to leave to start making phone calls and get things moving. Aurora felt herself wrenched into his enthusiasm, and whirled into a frenzy of excited activity. It was contagious and she let herself be carried away on his flow.

'I'll call you later. I love you,' he said hugging her again. He looked into her eyes, held her face in his hands and moved in close to her face as if he was going to kiss her, but instead, he brushed his lips against her cheek and her ear and then her neck, tingling every pore of her being as his breath stroked her soul. His touch meant everything, filling Aurora with a passionate burning. And then he left. The burning lingered for a few more seconds and then dissipated into the air along with his scent.

Displaced

How dare she threaten me when I have her best interests at heart!

And that upstart.

What does he think he's doing moving in on my wife?

Does he really think he can replace me? Her husband?

Did she think she could just walk away with the money?

She doesn't appreciate me.

She doesn't know what she's missing in me.

I was there for her through everything.

I supported her studies.

I supported her through her breakdown.

I had to take her away from her family.

I protected her.

I was the one she needed. Not them.

I know she loved me then.

She came to see me in hospital every day.

She watched over me.

I could tell they were getting to her.

They were using my accident as an excuse.

I could feel it.

A husband knows when his wife is being led astray.

My Hayabusa, destroyed.

Lost.

Aurora slipping away.
I have to get her back to where she was before.
When she loved me unconditionally.
When she never questioned my thinking or way of doing things.
When she showed me respect.
I shouldn't have allowed her to take all of those exams.
Accept those promotions.
The beginning of the end.
She started to think she was better than me.
Smarter.
Quicker.
Richer.
But then again...
It was good that we had that money coming in.
I could stretch out my convalescence.
Doctors never quite sure if I was improving (or faking).
They couldn't tell what my body was really doing.
Yes, the bones healed.
But there were twinges.
They had concerns.
The trauma that they couldn't measure.
The trauma they couldn't see.
And Aurora listened to their concerns.
She started to play her part as wife again.
Lying in hospital, I felt her return to me.
Slowly.
When I came home, Aurora did everything.
I kept her busy.

She had to show me her love.
Through her working days.
Through her cooking.
Through her shopping.
Through her cleaning.
Through her changing me.
Through her washing me.
Through her blowing me.
I made sure the cleaners and care assistants never stayed long.
I needed Aurora.
Not strangers.
I need Aurora.
She said she would call the police.
I need to find another way.
Hide.
Watch.
Wait.
Behind the screen, I can be anybody.
I can pretend.
I can capture.
I can bring her to me without her even knowing it.
I can destroy him.
She will return to me.
She will want me.
I will make her hate him.
MY WIFE.

*

When Aurora told her parents she was going away with Oliver, they were relieved and happy for her. She needed a break; she needed to be away from David. It was just a shame that she wouldn't have time to visit the family, as they had planned. Aurora said she was sure they could work it into the schedule while in Europe and if not, then she would just take some time out. It was what they wanted to hear.

Aurora's thoughts were now entirely driven by 'the tour' and she found Oliver's excitement and energy contagious. But there was a fear and trembling that she just couldn't allay. The tour would be an intense experience with them hurled together 24/7 with nowhere to escape to and always on call. She had glimpsed what that kind of world might look like for her. The constant attention, the constant need, no personal space, no time to think or breathe. Could she really cope with that? She had only just met Oliver, and despite feeling like she'd known him all of her life, the man with whom she spoke and the one she made love to was not the same man as the singer from Morpheme. They did not know each other well enough to be thrust together in such a way for so long. She wondered at her reticence now that she had had time to think. But everyone she had spoken to: Jennie, her parents, Jacqui, Kelly and Rachel had all said it was a great idea and an amazing opportunity. They had all mentioned she needed a holiday. She was unsure what that meant.

Her own career was catapulting her into an industry where she was already recognised for her work and in high demand. The more she actively worked in the pubs and clubs with up-and-coming bands, the more she was sought by established musicians who wanted to recapture the kudos of their breakthrough music by being interviewed by Aurora. Now she was well-known amongst those in the music industry, but not by the fans who were her audience and the readers of her work. It was a strange arrangement. Very different from the artist–fan relationship Oliver experienced. But she was happy with that. She wanted the career, the creative work that came out of working with creative people, not the fame, not that kind of publicity. She wanted to keep her privacy and enjoy her life in the shadows.

It had been a week since she'd been at the Dog and Duck with Oliver and since David had harassed her. David continued to haunt the back of her mind, but that power weakened as she realised his car no longer appeared outside her flat. Then Lesley called.

'How are you, Aurora?

'I'm fine, Lesley. Listen, I can't thank you enough for what you did for me. You really made a difference and I think it's scared David off. I haven't seen him or his car for days,' Aurora replied hastily, anticipating the reason for Lesley's call.

'I'm glad to hear it. But have you logged a complaint with the police yet?'

There was a pause.

'No, I haven't, yet. It's just been so busy and as David seems to have left, I don't think it's necessary.'

'Aurora!' said Lesley, incandescent with anger and frustration. Aurora knew then she was not going to get away with her feeble defence.

'I explained to you what happened to my sister. The way your ex-husband is behaving is not normal. You were terrified when you came into the shop and that reaction should be motivating you to report him. Do you really think he will just walk away suddenly after all this time?'

'Well, yes. Look, I think he will. Anyway, I'll be travelling soon, so I won't be here and he won't know where I am. I'll be surrounded by people. I'll be far away from here,' sighed Aurora. She felt as if her insides had been excavated, leaving a brittle shell about to crack. The hair-thin lines spreading, weakening, inactivating her ability to argue this away. Deep down, in those depths of subtle feelings that were easy to ignore, she could feel the nervous churning that she hadn't felt in such a long time. Recognising Lesley's concern for her didn't make her awareness any easier. It made the guilt heavier, like a lead weight, just adding to what she already felt about not being completely honest with her parents and not telling Oliver anything about David.

'That's not good enough, Aurora. Look, I know it's harsh and you can tell me it's not my business, but there is too much of that already going on. I'm going to report what I know about this incident to the police. And I really do care about what happens to you. But I won't let you just walk away, because one day you won't be walking anywhere,' whispered Lesley. Aurora could hear gasps of air and for a moment she thought she heard a single tear drop.

'Lesley, I'm really sorry. I had no idea how this was affecting you. I just feel so guilty about it all. I know it's stupid, I know it's not me, I know it's David and yet there is just this invisible power, an invisible hand that keeps me from taking any more action. I thought I was done with David after the divorce. I was hoping that would be the end of it. I will report it. I promise,' said Aurora.

'Don't let it be the last promise you make,' replied Lesley.

'I won't, and thank you for looking out for me. I'll let you know when I leave London.'

'Aurora, I'm sorry I was a bit harsh with you, but it's because I've seen what these kinds of people can do. They never just walk away. Please, do make the report. I'll leave you alone now,' Lesley replied slowly.

'I'll speak to you soon, Lesley. Bye.'

Aurora ended the call.

*

Aurora was rushing to Oliver's house. This was the first time she was seeing his place and she was excited and nervous. At times she imagined a large mansion with a butler, at other times it was a luxury apartment with an amazing view. As their relationship developed and there was more talk about 'the tour', she felt Oliver growing into the ideality. She felt as if she was losing him, the person she'd met at the gallery. She stepped out of Hampstead tube station to get her bearings. It was about a 20-minute walk to Oliver's address from there as there was no direct route, so she decided to take the park route. Turning right onto Heath Street, she walked towards Hampstead Heath Park. Aurora had never been to this part of London before. It had a lovely olde worlde village feel about it with independent shops, cafés and galleries opening up on both sides of her walk. Soon she was walking uphill into more leafy and residential parts. She turned onto West Heath Road and there was a duck pond acting as a roundabout. It was then a series of crossings, trying to find gaps in the traffic until she reached the other side of West Heath Road where there wasn't even a pavement to walk on. She walked and walked, feeling as if the trees and large houses were conspiring to stop her from finding Oliver. It was just gated green wall after gated green wall. Soon the largeness of the houses and the space they occupied had no effect on her, except to wish she had taken a taxi. She almost missed the small turning into the road where Oliver's house was. She walked up slowly, trying to work out the numbers and names of the houses. Eerily quiet, there were no human sounds, only the whispering trees and the noises of creatures used to having control of this environment. High brick walls and curving paths directed Aurora through the estate. She felt claustrophobic in this narrow backyard of the rich. Her phone was vibrating. It was Oliver.

'Do you want me to pick you up?'

'No, it's fine. I'm almost there. Remind me again of the number of your place.'

At that point, she looked around, realising she was standing right in front of Oliver's house. It was nothing like she had expected. So secluded, hidden, obscure. So unlike what she had thought Oliver was.

She rang the buzzer and the gate swung open. At that moment she wanted to run away. This was too alien to her. This was not her world, Anxiety screamed at her. How dare she think she could enter this arena? Who did she think she was? But it was too late. Oliver was running towards her, smiling, his eyes lit up like sunshine on sea—oh those eyes— and suddenly he was there with his arms wrapped around her, saying something Aurora couldn't understand, kissing Anxiety away. Except for the part of her very deep down. The shifting thing. That which would destroy what she had built out of spite. As she walked up the steps with Oliver towards his house, she kicked the thing back into its box. Today would not be that day.

'I'm so glad you're here. I'm so excited about working with you. Is this the first time you've been here?'

'Um, yes, it's the first time I've been to your house.' *Why did he not know that?*

'I've prepared some lunch in the back garden. We can eat, talk, relax a little before we get to work.'

'That sounds wonderful,' replied a relieved Aurora.

As they walked into his house, she could hear voices.

'Aurora's here, guys,' he shouted.

Aurora froze.

'What is it?' asked Oliver

Aurora took a deep breath.

'I didn't realise anyone else was going to be here. I thought it was just going to be us.' She looked helplessly at him.

'I thought I should introduce you to everyone. We can't sort out the tour dates without everyone else. Don't worry, they love you already. I told you, you are a musician's dream.' And he took her hand, squeezed it, and ever so gently pulled her into the kitchen.

'I don't think you've met the guys, but you should recognise them, even after the middle-age spread,' laughed Oliver.

'Speak for yourself, mate. Hi Aurora, it's great to meet you. Oliver hasn't stopped talking about you! I'm Matt. I guess it's been a while for all of us.' And he shook Aurora's hand.

Aurora relaxed.

'Great to meet you. Lead guitar, right?'

'Spot on. You see, Ollie, I haven't changed that much! I like Aurora even more.'

'And this is Craig,' said Oliver enjoying the badinage.

'Lovely to meet you, Aurora. So pleased you are working with us,' he said smiling and shaking Aurora's hand.

'It's lovely to meet you too, Craig. Drums, right?'

'Spot on.'

'You must remember me?'

'Um, bass guitar, Nathan?' exclaimed Aurora excitedly.

'I was worried there for a minute, but yeah. Great to meet you.'

'This is not a test, guys,' laughed Oliver.

'Do you mind?' And Aurora was suddenly enveloped in the arms of Nick, whom she instantly recognised. Aurora hugged him back, feeling silly and giddy.

'I'm Nick, keyboard, and a big fan of your writing,' he whispered.

'OK, guys. Give it a rest now, would you?' Oliver was a little piqued by his bandmates.

'Aurora, let me introduce you to Chris and Robin.' And Oliver took Aurora outside into the amazing back garden.

Aurora had never seen anything like it. While not huge, it reminded her of the Lost Gardens of Heligan. There were tree sculptures, a small pond bordered by all shades and shapes of greenery, flows of green and purple draped over walls and wooden frames, mosses of all shades and a controlled wildness Aurora had never seen in a garden before. There was a large patio with wooden furniture, a coal barbeque, brick oven and a wide wooden serving area with everything required to cook outside.

And standing over the barbeque were a man and a woman.

'Robin, Chris, this is Aurora.'

They both turned around, greeting Aurora with smiles and welcomes.

'So, you're the famous journalist who's managed to get Morpheme back on tour!' said Chris.

'I wouldn't call myself a famous journalist. And I'm certainly *not* responsible for this reunion. As great as it is, I can't claim any credit,' replied Aurora wondering what Oliver had been telling people.

'Well, it's lovely to meet the lady who has put this egotist in his place. I'm Chris, by the way.'

'Chris has been my manager for decades and is a trusted advisor—although granted I haven't always listened to his advice,' replied Oliver winking. 'And this is Robin, our tour manager. This is the first time Robin is working with us, so I have to behave. She has amazing experience, so we are very lucky she agreed to work with us on this.

'Thanks for the great intro. It's lovely to meet you, Aurora,' said Robin, shaking Aurora's hand.

'You too. I have to say, I'm a bit overwhelmed. I wasn't expecting to meet anyone today.'

'Oliver loves surprising people, but it's usually in the wrong way,' said Chris.

'OK, OK, don't put Aurora off the idea of coming with us. Let's eat and then we can discuss dates.'

'I need to freshen up,' said Aurora.

Oliver smiled and led Aurora by the hand upstairs. Aurora felt eyes watching her.

'Come and use my bathroom. Are you OK? You seem a bit quiet.'

'I'm just overwhelmed really. I wish you'd told me this was going to be a meeting. I thought it was just going to be us looking at dates together,' said Aurora, exasperated.

'Sorry, I should have asked you. I was just so excited you said yes. I didn't want to waste time. You're not too upset with me, are you?' pleaded Oliver.

Aurora looked down. How could she answer that? She was really pissed off and yet... Oliver's excitement was contagious.

He stroked her face and pulled her chin up to him. Looking into her eyes, he saw the fire and anger there. But it didn't scare him, that was what he wanted. She still had that passion and fire for life within her and it would push her to get the best out of him and the band when they went on tour. He bent down to take her lips into his, ever so softly. The way he knew it turned her on.

Aurora looked into Oliver's deep blue eyes and tried to find the Oliver she had fallen in love with. She struggled to find him at that moment. She wasn't sure if it was because she was still angry with him or because she saw a new aspect of him she didn't like. What did he want from her? As he bent down to kiss her, the angry fire within her flashed again. She responded to his kiss, but only through numb lips. Aurora extracted herself to go to the bathroom.

Finding herself in confusion again, her attitude shifted. She knew she had to make this a success, at least for the work. She couldn't understand this Oliver and at this moment, she didn't want to make the effort. She really wanted to run away; place all her insecurities that she hadn't had since David in a box, and kick it away. But there were people downstairs, there was Jennie, and there were her parents. So many people willing her to make this opportunity work. Sighing, she checked her face, ran her fingers through her hair and thought, fuck it!

*

'There you are,' shouted Oliver. 'Come and sit down. We're going to eat.'

Aurora smiled wryly and sat down where she was told to sit.

She sat at a large table. Oliver had placed her opposite him at the other end. He seemed to be enjoying his status. Aurora had to pull herself out of this hole she had fallen into. It wasn't that she was ignoring Oliver's behaviour, she would bring that up with him later. It was much more about what she wanted from this. She seemed to have been swept up in all the euphoria and excitement without really thinking about it from her perspective. What did she want from Oliver? They were no longer the fan–artist communion. Their relationship had developed beyond that, she thought. And yet, Aurora was feeling the creeping of some distance in their relationship, evolving as it was influenced by external factors.

Food was being passed around the table. Aurora mindlessly added everything onto her plate. Wine was doing the rounds as well, but Aurora declined politely. Everyone was chatting, laughing, joking, reminiscing, harmonising without her.

'I find these kind of meetings a bit loud, don't you?' asked Nick as he leaned closer to Aurora.

'Is it that obvious?' asked Aurora.

'You're fine. Luckily we have several people here who like the sound of their own voices, so we can hide in the background,' he smiled, winking at her.

Aurora suddenly relaxed. Flashes of music videos pulled Nick out of the shadows and she smiled. Yes, she liked Nick, so she asked him, 'Do you mind me asking how you got involved with this? I thought you guys hadn't spoken in years.'

'I don't mind at all. No, we didn't talk for a long time. I was sick of touring and sick of deadlines. I missed my family and I'd had enough. For some reason, all my frustrations and exhaustion were directed at the guys, but it was just the situation we were in. We were so scared we would lose a deal, lose our reputation and everything else we had worked so hard for, that it kept us going until enough was enough. When I returned home to an empty house, the realisation hit me that I had no life. I blamed everyone else, especially Oliver, as I could tell he really enjoyed that life. I thought he had kept pushing us with the record company. So, I cut off everyone I worked with. It needed to be done. There was no other way of us moving on and getting to this point. A few years ago, I ran into Craig and we chatted about everything. It was cathartic for both of us. We started meeting up regularly and playing together. That was nice. We could just play what we wanted and soon we started working on new material together. Nothing like the Morpheme sound, but a couple of those pieces are making it into the new album. That was a rather long answer, but I guess I should get used to that with you coming with us on tour. Do you mind if I ask you how you got involved? I've read your articles and they're great. Don't get me wrong, but this all seems a bit quick.' Nick was staring at Aurora, searching for an answer. Was he questioning her legitimacy?

'You have every right to ask me. It *is* a bit sudden and quick and although I guess this is my job now, I had no idea that this tour would be happening. I took Oliver to one of the live band pubs I go to. The pub manager has a real ear for spotting talent, so it's always a great place to see up-and-coming musicians. I had to work and Oliver came with me. Someone recognised him and that was that. I could see him in the crowd, having photos taken and signing beer mats. He was loving the attention. Up until that point, the Oliver I knew intimately was quiet, thoughtful and withdrawn but witty and interesting too. Suddenly, he turned into the rock star and I felt I lost him. I'm saying too much. You don't need to hear all of this.'

'You can tell me anything. It won't go back to Ollie. One thing I will say about him, he always has everyone's best interests at heart, but they are dictated by his motivations. He will always try to convince you that his wants align with yours, but he usually gets his way.' Nick squeezed Aurora's shoulder. His touch was both comforting and distressing. She smiled, unable to shake the feeling that there was something else. His touch reminded her of another touch, but she couldn't place it.

'Ladies and gentlemen, and I use that term loosely,' shouted Chris, standing up and holding a glass of wine in preparation of a toast. Craig ran round the table refilling everyone's glasses in readiness, 'I'd like to say I am so pleased we are here together to bring back one of the greatest bands on this planet. I've known you guys for a long time now and I know this is going to be an amazing tour. And I know we have one person to thank for this, so please raise your glasses to Aurora.'

Everyone toasted Aurora. She sat and smiled weakly, raising her glass in reply. Oliver smiled his intense smile at her, his blue eyes flashing, willing her to want this as much as he did. Then it was all over and everyone went back to their conversations.

Nick suddenly shouted out to Oliver, 'So, do you think you'll be able to handle the girls better, Ollie? They're going to be a bit older than they were the first time around.'

Oliver flashed a curled smile in response. He didn't want to discuss this in front of Aurora.

'I don't think it will be an issue this time. We were all young in those days. You had your fair share of girls as I recall?'

'You're right, of course. But you're going to have to behave yourself this time round.'

'I don't think it's about behaving myself. I'm excited about Aurora coming with us. This tour is going to be very different from those we've done in the past. And Aurora is an integral part of that. Anyway, the fans will be older too. We won't have the same issues. I hope not, anyway.'

'I don't know, Oliver, some of the fan blogs out there are pretty scary. I think it's a whole new ball game and we can't be complacent. You can't know who some of these fans behind the blogs are. Will they turn up to a gig in person? Will they want special attention? You know now everything can be recorded. You just have to be so careful. Personally, I think we should just keep the interaction on stage and not risk the in-person signings like we used to do,' said Matt.

'Guys, you're gonna have the best security on this tour, so you don't need to worry. We can arrange anything for you,' added Chris.

'Aurora, what do you think we should do? I mean, it was fine when we were at the pub together,' said Oliver.

Everyone looked at Aurora.

'Well... that was different though, no one was expecting you to be there. It was impromptu and it was only one fan who recognised you initially. I think going back out on tour, coming back into the limelight, as it were, you could make yourselves targets for those fans who want to re-live moments from their past. You don't just have the music and the interaction now; you have a fan base who feel they have a shared history with you. I feel that, too, to some degree. When I listen to your music now, it brings back a lot of those memories. It isn't a contemporary experience anymore and that adds a layer to the relationship you have with your fans.'

'But you know I don't agree with that, Aurora,' interjected Oliver. 'Fans don't have those rights over me or the band. There *is* no relationship.'

'Oh, but there *is,* Oliver. I understand what you're saying, but things are different now.'

'She's right, you know, Ollie,' said Chris.

'You're going to have to start making videos and posting updates to entice the fans. Everyone will expect you to do this. Otherwise, you just won't get the numbers, no matter how loyal you think your fans are,' said Aurora.

'Why do we need to do this? Why should any of us have to expose our lives to the outer world?' asked Nathan.

'Because that is what fans expect. The more you can bring them into your inner world, the more they will pay for video content, for your music. We're talking downloads now. There is no chart based on singles and albums sales like there used to be. For some fans, it's you, not even your music, but *you*, who are the content that they want to possess,' replied Chris, almost exasperated at how old-fashioned their thinking was. He would have to speak to Aurora to get Oliver on side with this.

'This is bullshit,' said Nathan standing up suddenly.

'Yeah, it is. And I hate it,' added Oliver.

'It's how you're going to have to navigate this tour. Do you still want to do it?' asked Aurora looking round the table.

Matt, Craig and Nick nodded sheepishly. Nathan and Oliver looked at each other.

'Chris, can't we get someone to do this crap *for* us?' asked Nathan.

'Aurora can do it. She understands this type of marketing and we can trust her. Besides, I've promised her completely exclusive material so *she* gets what she needs and *we* can get some respite from the marketing,' said Oliver.

'But it's better coming directly from you guys. The fans can tell when it's someone else's voice behind the content,' said Chris.

'Look, I've done a little bit of this kind of work recently,' said Robin. 'I can work with Aurora on this. I think it's a lot to ask for her to do this alone,' she added.

'Thank God,' said Nathan. 'I don't think I could cope with having my downtime taken away from me. Thanks, Robin. And Aurora.'

Aurora looked at Oliver. She didn't recognise the man in front of her. She understood his point of view, but when she had seen him with the fans in the Dog and Duck, she was sure he was in his element. He craved the adulation, the attention, the attraction. And he had just allocated her as a social media junior. That was *not* what she had signed up to.

'OK everyone, we really need to do some work now. Let's get on with the task in hand, please,' said Robin as she stood up.

They all meandered into the lounge. The atmosphere had changed and Aurora wondered if this was how it was going to be on tour: euphoria one moment and then pure negativity the next.

Aurora walked through with Robin, who had been quick to grab Aurora's arm and chat with her separately.

'Are you OK?'

'Yes, why?' asked Aurora. Damn! Was it so obvious?

'You seem a little perturbed.'

'I may be a bit confused by Oliver's reaction to this. When I saw him in the pub with all of those people, he looked like he was revelling in it. And I genuinely think he missed all of that, so I don't understand where he's coming from now. It made sense when we discussed this when we first met, but now I'm wondering about his motivations for the tour. He still has a successful single music career, so he doesn't really need the tour. I'm nervous that there is something else,' said Aurora.

Robin squeezed her arm.

'Ours is not to reason why but to do as we are asked,' she said and smiled at Aurora.

Aurora was not amused by this comment. She didn't want to be controlled again. She wanted full disclosure before taking such a big decision. Everyone seemed to have a hidden agenda—well, hidden from her anyway.

'We need to work together to whip these guys into shape. I know I can rely on you. If Oliver goes along with an idea, then the others will follow. Nick may delay and complain for a little bit, but he always toes the line.'

'You seem to know them very well. I thought Oliver said this was the first time you're working with them?'

'Yes, it is, but I've been in the industry for over 20 years. I've spoken to others who've worked with them on tour in the past. I know what's coming. It helps me manage the band so I can manage the tour. You look shocked?'

'I just didn't anticipate you being quite so… business like,' replied Aurora. She suddenly felt as if she had fallen into another world she couldn't escape from. There was no going back.

As Oliver was bringing in the coffee and tea, Aurora was seated in an armchair as if she were a naughty child.

'Thanks Oliver. Right guys, get a drink and then I want you all to focus. No one is going anywhere until we have our plan in place,' ordered Robin.

Decouple

'Hi. How are you?' asked Aurora as she leaned past the table to hug Rachel and John.

'We're good. So good to see you, Aurora,' John replied.

'It's been so long and I feel like I've abandoned you,' said Aurora, concerned.

'Don't be silly. We know you're busy and it hasn't stopped for us either. If anything, we owe you,' smiled Rachel.

'How are the guys?' asked Aurora.

'We're all good. You know we're going on tour now? So only a few more weeks and that will be us on the move for the next 18 months. Everything has happened so quickly. But you know what, this is what we wanted,' replied John.

'Aurora, we can't thank you enough for your support. No, really, very few bands get this kind of exposure at the beginning of their careers. As a band we were always confident we could make a successful career out of music, but you speeded up that journey by years,' said Rachel emphatically.

The waiter arrived to take their order.

'Aurora, we wanted to ask you a favour,' said John looking directly at Aurora.

'Ask away,' she replied.

'Would you come on tour with us? You know, like a mentor, and also as our biographer, if you like? We could really use your support.'

'We know it's short notice,' jumped in Rachel, 'but we didn't have details until recently and we really wanted to ask you in person. You look upset. Are we asking too much?' she asked fearfully.

The waiter brought their drinks.

'No, no. I am so flattered and honoured you've asked me. And had you asked me a couple of weeks ago, I would have said yes, but I have some news as well. I'm going on tour with Morpheme. It's not for a few months yet—we only confirmed the dates this week—but I'm committed to that now. I'm really sorry. I would love to have gone with you.'

'With Morpheme?' asked John. 'But that's incredible, I didn't even know they were getting back together. How?'

'Well, that's a long story, but I may have had a bit of involvement in it—purely by accident though. They were my favourite band when I was in my teens. My friends and I were really into them then. And their music still evokes emotions in me. But I met Oliver recently by accident and it went from there,' Aurora said quietly, hoping her affair with Oliver wouldn't show on her face.

John and Rachel swapped a quick glance at each other. Was there something else Aurora wasn't telling them?

'I know I'm pushing this, but could we convince you to come out to us while we're on tour for a few days at least?'

asked Rachel. 'We can work around you. We've tried to work in some rest weeks for the band and tour team over the 18 months.'

'Send me the dates you're thinking about and I'll look at my diary and get back to you. But I'm sure we can make this work, somehow,' replied Aurora smiling.

Their food arrived steaming and hot and wafting an aroma to wet their appetites. They tucked into it as they shared their hopes for the band, their insecurities and their warmth for each other.

*

Aurora's life was finally at the stage she had always wanted it to be. She was fully in control (even if it didn't feel like it) and her career was taking a trajectory unlike anything she had experienced in her life before. Her relationship with Oliver was solid. He had sought her out after the meeting at his house and whisked her away for a long weekend in Rome. It was just what she needed. The two of them together, with space and time to indulge in each other, discover fantasies, tastes and hopes for the future. And Oliver had said 'their future'. Aurora had shuddered (she didn't understand why), but then a euphoria had set in as Oliver's hands had slid around her waist and he'd whispered that he loved her.

How long had it been since she had felt such emotions? She had forgotten the feeling of passion and warm love.

They had not existed in her recent life, having been expunged decades ago. But now, life was beautiful! It was... she didn't want to say the word; it would bring disaster. She wasn't superstitious, but just in case...

Aurora's parents were with family in Italy, happy and safe in the knowledge that Aurora would soon be travelling. Things seemed to have resolved themselves. Aurora had called Jacqui and the others from her NSM Team. Everyone was doing well in their new jobs and they had all had an FCA letter confirming they would soon be receiving compensation.

Aurora's work was really getting some good traction online now, particularly in the last few weeks when she'd noticed her website content was going viral. Everything was just so 'perfect'. There, she'd said it.

Her calendar was filling up as she finalised her dates to join The Forum while they were touring Germany. She would fly into Munich, stay with The Forum for a day there and then travel with them by train to Berlin for two days. They wanted to have fun in Berlin: explore the underground tunnels and the KitKat Club. Aurora wasn't sure how she felt about that, but she would deal with that when she got there. She might even surprise herself.

Oliver was a little despondent over losing Aurora for a few days. He was now so attentive, but Aurora was pleased to be doing something else. She didn't want to use the word escaping.

Aurora was at home. It was a quiet week. She had deliberately blanked out her diary to leave herself some breathing space between all her work commitments and planning. Her treat was to spend the day reading and watching films. No input from her required, she would just passively absorb someone else's output. Wonderful! She relaxed on the sofa. Film on. Glass of fresh lemonade and some naughty Green & Black's white chocolate.

Then her phone pinged. She ignored it. Another ping. And another. Soon it was obvious something was happening. Email and social media notifications had set her phone alight. So she picked up her mobile and read her screen. There were over a hundred notifications and her phone was still screaming. She didn't understand it. As far as she had understood, Morpheme's return tour wouldn't be made public until the following week. She read through the notifications. She was trying to comprehend what was happening as pop-ups attacked her screen. Suddenly, she did understand. Someone had posted something about her affair with Oliver. But how had they found out? What was going on? Suddenly, she saw photos of herself appearing in the online articles and links. Her name linked with Oliver's. And it just kept going. More explicit photos of her on a beach in her underwear. She turned off the volume, but her screen continued to flash the incriminating photographs. Some of the photographs were incomprehensible. Oliver and Aurora together, but not in any way that she recognised them together. They only had a few private photographs.

Her phone flashed an incoming call. It was Oliver.

'Have you seen what's happening online? It's incredible!'

'Yes, I didn't say anything to anyone. I don't know where this has come from. I think some of the photos are fake. I'm really sorry. I just don't know how this has happened,' Aurora replied, frightened by what this would mean for their real life relationship.

'Are you kidding? We couldn't have asked for better publicity before the reunion tour announcement. I thought you had leaked this as a publicity stunt,' exclaimed an excited Oliver.

'What! How could you think I would resort to something so low and cheap to get attention? This is not me. How do you think my parents are going to react to this? This is uncontrollable. And I never wanted our relationship in the public domain. I can't afford that.'

'What do you mean?'

'I mean, I don't need my ex-husband knowing about my private life. He already suspected I was seeing you. This is not what I signed up for. Now I've become your "woman", my writing will never be taken seriously again.'

'Is it really so bad for you to be associated with me?'

'No, but... don't make this into a question of how I feel about you. This is not what this is.' Then she paused. 'Oh my God! It was you. *You* released this!'

'Aurora, it wasn't me. You know, I am excited by this. This kind of publicity is so different from what we had in the 80s and 90s, but I would never leak anything about us and

I wouldn't talk about our relationship to anyone without speaking to you first. You know that, deep down.'

'Yes,' whispered Aurora. She knew it as soon as Oliver admitted his excitement.

'But, who then? I've been so careful. I didn't want the tour compromised.'

'Well, I can tell you it's not the guys and not Chris or Robin. They are completely focused on the tour and don't want anything to interfere with it. They wouldn't step outside of the tour plan. Maybe we need to have a look at the posts and try to figure out where this started from. I'll come over.' And before Aurora could reply, Oliver had disappeared from her phone.

The notifications continued. She tried to find the first few posts. They were just social media posts initially. She opened each link to drill down into each one and found an account named HayabusaFan101. Aurora switched off her television and sat at her desk. She took an A4 writing pad and red pen and started listing the posts: date, time, account name, keywords (her name, Oliver's name, Morpheme). Slowly, a pattern started to emerge from two accounts, HayabusaFan101 and another account that seemed to copy the HayabusaFan101 content: WatchingYouNow1970. A shiver ran down her spine when all of a sudden, the buzzer rang, making her jump. She took a deep breath and pressed the button to let Oliver in.

Something about the accounts made her feel uneasy, but she wasn't sure what it was. From what she could see in the short time she had dissected the posts, it was clear this had been planned and it was a fairly sophisticated campaign. But who was behind it, and why? What did they gain, apart from a few extra likes and connections on their social media accounts?

There was a knock at the door. What now? She was still trying to work out what the angle on this was when she opened the door. And in walked David, who closed the door behind him, quickly grabbing her and covering her mouth so she wouldn't scream.

Aurora's heart beat in protest and fear, feeling like it would explode out of her chest as David squeezed her tightly. She knew she had to relax and had to keep David calm. She slowed her breathing down and composed herself. David loosened his grip as he felt her muscles give way to his hold.

'Good girl,' he whispered in her ear, closing his eyes as he breathed in her smell. Now he realised what he had really missed.

'Now, you will behave yourself, won't you?' he asked, nudging his chin and nose into her cheek.

It had been soft and sweet when they were young, but now all Aurora could feel was his stubble scratching her skin and his chin bone digging into her face. She wanted to recoil in disgust, but had to maintain what was left of her composure.

'How is the writing career going?' asked David as he released Aurora, turning her to face him.

She realised he had some kind of cloth wrapped around his hand.

'It's going well, thank you,' she faltered. Every word felt like it was scraping off a layer of her skin.

'Good. I'm glad. I can make things even better for you, you know. I am quite powerful now. I have contacts. You don't need that idiot in your life. Especially now that he's put you in this impossible position.'

'David, what are you talking about?'

'All that social media stuff about you and him and what you do to him. Haven't you seen it?'

'No. I try not to use social media.'

'Liar!' he snarled as he nodded towards her computer screen. It was still open to a cyber world advertising her and Oliver's relationship.

'David, what do you want from me?' cried Aurora, exhausted. It occurred to her that she might not see her parents or Oliver again. Lesley's warnings flashed red across her vision as she swayed. The floor was moving violently. She reached out towards the sofa to sit down.

'What's wrong? Do you want some water?' asked David, rushing to her, his dark face too close for comfort.

'Yes, please,' replied Aurora as she took a deep breath. She needed to escape. But how? How could she be in this position? This didn't happen in real life. This wasn't happening to her. She had buried this shit in her life. And yet here it was in full corpse glory: David, zombie-like, pursuing her until the very end.

He brought her a glass of water and watched her sip it. He reached out, pushing the bottom of the glass up, forcing the full glass of water down her throat. She spluttered and tried to regain control. She realised he was capable of anything and had come prepared for any eventuality or ending. She trembled at the thought of her parents having to see her dead at the hands of David, after everything he had put them through.

Slowly, the fear turned and burned into anger. Anger at David's presumption. How dare he treat her like this? What the hell gave him any rights over her? Her anger fired her up as she filled with rage, not just for herself and her parents, but for every victim who had had their rights violated by another.

'Why are you here, David?' said Aurora as she stood up.

'I'm here to get you back. I love you, Aurora. We belong together,' he smiled weakly.

'You don't own me. I have choices. I make my own decisions. I don't want to go with you. Do you understand? I will never go back to you,' she shouted.

David moved towards her, hand raised. But Aurora was quicker and moved behind the sofa. David noted the shift in his disadvantage. His face darkened until he really did start to resemble a zombie with dead skin and eyes. It was his eyes that Aurora noticed the most. Almost black. Dead, like coal. No reasoning with him. No empathy. Just his madness. Aurora would have to remove herself physically. She now knew she couldn't talk her way out of this situation.

'Come on, Aurora. It wasn't all bad, surely? We loved each other once. I still love you. Can't you give me something at least? Something of yourself, a promise?'

'No, David. No. I can't promise you anything. And you shouldn't ask me. If you loved me the way you say you do, you wouldn't be harassing me and treating me like this,' she replied as she gestured with her arms to deflect from her inching backwards towards the door.

'But you won't listen to me. I know what you need in your life. You are making mistake after mistake. Do you really think that idiot is in love with you? Don't you know he was the one who spread those lies about you. How can you be in love with him after this?'

Aurora froze with the realisation of who was really behind the posts. His statement was an admission of guilt. And David saw from Aurora's reaction that she knew it was him. Damn! It had seemed like such a perfect plan. She would have blamed and hated Oliver for this and come running back to him. But now that dream was scarred with reality and he would now have to take the alternative route.

'David, you need to leave. Now. There is no other way this can end,' said Aurora pointing at the door. She was only centimetres away from reaching the lock.

'OK, I'll leave. But you're coming with me. I'm not leaving without you, Aurora. You get to choose how you leave: conscious or *un*conscious. I don't have time to waste now. You've wasted enough of our time with this nonsense divorce and separation.' David moved towards Aurora. She was almost within reach of her freedom.

Just then the buzzer screamed at them both. David panicked. The noise was unexpected and alarmed him. But Aurora pulled the door open and slipped out of David's grasp. She ran down the corridor, pushed open the stairwell door and ran down the stairs, shouting for help.

'Aurora?' shouted a voice from somewhere below.

'Oliver?'

Oliver looked up the stairwell and saw Aurora on the floor above him. Then David appeared on Aurora's floor.

'Aurora,' shouted David with such fierceness it froze her where she was.

'Run!' shouted Oliver. Aurora ran down, jumping two stairs at a time. Oliver grabbed her hand and they ran out of the block of flats. The taxi Oliver had come in was still there and they jumped in and locked the doors.

'Take a photo of the man that runs out of that door,' shouted Oliver at the taxi driver.

'What? Why?'

'Do it now! I'll pay you.'

'Please,' shouted Aurora.

David rushed out of the main door, disorientated by the brightness of the afternoon light. He couldn't see Aurora anywhere. The taxi driver took a couple of photos, then Oliver told him to drive back to the pick-up address. David looked around and saw Aurora in the vehicle. Approaching like an angry bull, he descended on the passenger side and started punching the window.

The taxi driver suddenly realised the seriousness of the situation and started the car, but David wouldn't move and continued to try to smash the window.

'Drive!' shouted Oliver.

At that point, the driver quickly turned the car and sped past David, who ran after them.

Aurora and Oliver turned to each other in relief.

'Are you OK?' he asked Aurora, holding onto her as if he would never let her go.

'Yes, I need to talk to the police,' she replied while staring ahead.

Oliver told the taxi driver to drive to the nearest police station where they all gave their statements.

Aurora sat in the waiting room while Oliver finished off his statement. She held an untouched cup of tea. What had just happened?

*

Oliver took Aurora back to his house.

'Drink this,' said Oliver handing Aurora a glass of brandy.

'I don't want it,' she said, pushing the glass away.

'You should have something to warm you up inside,' he replied curtly, leaving the glass on the table in front of her.

Aurora looked at Oliver as he walked out of her view into the kitchen.

Something had broken. Was it her? Had David finally won after all these years of trying to reclaim her instinct, herself, stand up in her own right as a human being and not as an appendage to another, not as an afterthought? But now?

Oliver returned to the room and sat down next to her on the sofa. His face had softened as he convinced her to at least take a sip of the drink he'd offered.

It burned through her to dull the anxiety still lingering in every nerve ending. But she didn't want her senses to be dulled into a fog. She wanted to feel the pain, wanted to experience how her body was coping with its fight or flight responses. It is what keeps us alive. This what she had ignored in herself for so many years and David was the consequence of that ignorance. She pushed the glass away.

'How are you feeling now?' asked Oliver distantly.

'I'd be lying if I said I was OK. I guess I'm still in shock. But I want to feel the shock. I don't want to get drunk. I just can't believe it. You know, Lesley and Jennie warned me about his behaviour and I just brushed it away. I never thought David was capable of something like this. And that is the trouble, I didn't think. Had I paid attention to my own experience with David, I would have done something sooner. For God's sake, I left him twice. I should have seen this coming.'

'I wish you'd told me about him,' said Oliver leaning forward and placing his hand gently on Aurora's back.

'He was supposed to be relegated to my history. There was no reason to discuss him, well, certainly not his behaviour. And to be honest, we just haven't had that kind of conversation. We haven't really talked, have we? I don't know that much about your previous relationships either. Maybe now's the time to be having that conversation?'

'Isn't it a bit late?'

'What do you mean?' asked Aurora shuddering.

'Just that. David has happened. There is no point in talking about him now. We need to move on. We have other priorities now.'

Aurora looked at Oliver.

'Is that what I am to you? Is it just the tour and the writing that you want from me?' asked Aurora, her voice cracking. She coughed to clear her throat, but it was no use, anxiety and stress were constricting her throat, like ghostly hands around her neck.

'You know that's not true. I just don't see the point in talking things over all the time. It's just better to deal with things and move on. Look, Aurora, I'll be honest with you, despite all the madness of touring over the years and dealing with some unhinged fans, I have never felt as scared as I did today. As I was giving the police my statement, it dawned on me that I know nothing about you or your past life and I don't want to. I live in the moment and for the future. The past causes too many problems. Just cut it off.'

'No. You can't just ignore the past. My past has made me the person I am today, the person I thought you were in love with. Hopefully?'

'No, it's your attitude to life that makes you the person I'm in love with. And I *am* in love with you. But I'm not good at this emotional stuff. It scares me. It's something I can't control. And if I can't control it, there is no point in my getting involved in it.'

'You sound like David,' whispered Aurora.

'Is that what you think of me?'

'Don't twist my words. You're talking about controlling. Life isn't about controlling emotions or relationships. I don't understand you. You say you live in the moment, for the future, but you can't control that either. You go with what's happening in that moment.'

'But it feels different; it's not baggage. It's exciting and exhilarating. You know, that's why I fell in love with you. You had so much energy and passion. I mean, to start a brand-new career from scratch, that takes balls. And I loved that in you. The fact you just happened to be working in the same industry as me was a bonus. I could and can *still* see so much potential for our relationship. I want to look to our future. Not the past.'

Aurora hung her head in her hands. She was finding this too difficult. Oliver kept referring to having loved her, but then talking about their future. The ground was shifting again. Her world was morphing into her blue and green nightmares. She couldn't stay here with him. It was an uneven battleground for this kind of discussion. She needed Oliver to concede something to her, even if he didn't agree with her view. He should respect her perspective, not drown it out.

'I'm going to stay with Jennie. I need to have some time alone,' she said standing up. The ground dropped back into place.

'You can stay here as long as you like. I want you here,' said Oliver standing up with Aurora and wrapping his arms around her. Was that all he thought she needed?

'No. I know you want me here, but I just need some time alone. To reset.'

'OK, fine. Call me when you get to Jennie's. Do you want me to drop you off?'

'No, thanks. I'll call Jennie. She'll come and pick me up.'

Oliver hugged Aurora again and disappeared, leaving her alone.

'Jennie, I need your help. Are you busy now?'

'Aurora, what's happened? No, not busy, just tell me what you need. Where are you? Is it David?'

'I'm at Oliver's place. Can you pick me up from here?'

'Of course. Send me the address. What's happened? You're worrying me.'

'I'll tell you more when we meet, but it *is* to do with David. I need to go back to my flat and pick up a few things, but can I come and stay with you and Mike for a few days? I know it's last minute and I'll keep out of your way, but I just need to be around friends,' said Aurora trembling. She wouldn't be able to hold it in for much longer.

'I'm on my way.'

Denial

When they finally reached Jennie's house, Mike was there waiting to give Aurora a big hug. It was what she needed. Genuine affection and support from someone she trusted. It had been a long day and Aurora realised she hadn't eaten at all. But there were no pangs of hunger. Only an emotional exhaustion she had not expected to experience again. She thought she had learned to control her world, but once again David had crushed that myth. Would she ever be rid of him? Her past never seemed to leave her. Or was it that she hadn't dealt with the past? Truthfully and secretly to herself she finally acknowledged she had ignored these issues. Suddenly, she wondered about the other issues that would resurface. What else was lurking in the recesses of her mind?

They had left Aurora to sleep for a couple of hours. Jennie had repeated Aurora's story to Mike and he was horrified. Not just by David's actions, but by Oliver's response to Aurora. He wanted to call Oliver to tell him what he thought about him, but Jennie held him back, talking him out of it while feeling a warmth come over her for Mike. He would always surprise her with a reaction so that she fell even more in love with him. She knew how lucky she was to have him in her life.

When Aurora came out of the bedroom, she could smell a wonderful aroma of seafood and smoke. Mike was cooking on the barbecue when Jennie saw Aurora. It was still light, but the sun was past its zenith, allowing a coolness to flow through the air.

'I was just about to come and knock on the door,' smiled Jennie. 'How are you feeling? You must be hungry by now?'

'I'm fine. Still a little shaken really. I'm unsure about how I should feel or what I should do next. I guess I still feel in limbo,' replied Aurora, smiling weakly. She didn't want Jennie to worry.

'Well, come and eat a little at least. Look, Mike's cooked lobster,' said Jennie seating Aurora.

There was a wonderful array of food: mixed salad, tabbouleh, vegetable skewers, mayonnaise with lemon and pepper, wild mushroom carpaccio, ciabatta and an array of Mediterranean condiments. And then Mike served the barbecued lobster, cooked to perfection. With it he poured glasses of a chilled Domaine des Tourelles Rosé, squeezing Aurora's shoulder as he walked around the table.

The sound of cracking lobster shells brought back a bit of reality to Aurora. Sitting in the fresh air with her friends, life felt good again. For a little while.

Aurora ate and drank. The lobster was meaty and soft, offering the bittersweet aroma of its flesh seared in smoking coals, the vegetables crisp and honeyed while the tabbouleh was herby and tart in contrast. Aurora's senses were on fire after the dulling effect of the day.

As they sat and drank, resting and leaving only empty dishes, they watched the sun start to set across the garden.

'You can tell me to sod off, but I hope you're going to dump that idiot rock star,' said Mike.

'Mike, you promised not to say anything,' interrupted Jennie.

'Well, I can't *not* say anything, can I? Aurora, you're our friend and we really care about you. After everything you've been through, do you really need to stay with an insensitive prick like that?'

'Aurora, ignore him, the wine's gone to his head,' Jennie said glaring at Mike while she cleared the table.

Aurora stood up to take some dishes inside.

'Thanks, Mike. I know you care. You and Jennie have done more than you can possibly imagine for me already. But I need to sort Oliver out myself. I can't just walk away. That seems to be his tactic. I thought a lot about this. I ignored all the signs regarding David and I don't want to make the same mistake with Oliver. One way or another, our relationship needs to be defined and resolved.'

'I don't know why women put up with so much shit from men. Well, if that's what you want to do, you know we're both here for you and if you want me to speak to him, you know, the macho bullshit thing, man to man, just let me know. I promise to restrain myself,' he said winking.

'I'm sure you *would* restrain yourself. And I appreciate the offer,' replied Aurora as she smiled at him.

With cardigans, coffee, biscotti and bowls of berries, they returned to the garden. There was a calmness around them as they watched the purple sky.

'You know you can stay with us as long as you need to and I'm not chasing you away, but what are you going to do tomorrow?' asked Jennie.

Aurora sighed.

'I don't know. I just don't know. I know I should, but I feel like my world has shifted again. What I thought is all wrong. I'm scared and tired. I guess, I should phone the police to see what's happening with David. Oh God. I just want it all to be over.'

Jennie knelt in front of Aurora to hug her. Aurora took her willingly and hugged her tight. The feeling overwhelmed her, tears escaped, and emotions surfaced frantically, as if she were swimming to the surface for air. Jennie held Aurora's trembling frame, absorbing the pain, until she could take Aurora to bed to lay her exhausted body down.

*

Aurora was surrounded by green mist. She existed. But she stood nowhere. There was only the mist enveloping, caressing, stroking her. She felt the touch of a hand, the soft fingers lingering over her lips, the hand holding her face, her cheek encompassed within the palm. She closed her eyes, falling into the hand. A finger drew a line down her throat, her chest, in between her breasts. A naked realisation made her feel vulnerable. The green mist shrouded her, only the hand was there, wanting her, making her ache with its touch. All she could do was react, give herself. As she opened her eyes, she saw the hand extend into an arm, shoulder, chest, face. Harry's face. Aurora gasped and wanted to scream. Harry brought his finger up to his lips. Shhhhhhh. He placed his other finger on Aurora's lips.

She couldn't think why she was terrified of Harry. Why did she feel so scared? Harry was naked in his 18-year-old body. Aurora was in her 49-year-old body. The mist started to thin as a faint light, like sun-stroked clouds, filtered through. Slowly, Aurora noticed the marks on Harry's body: bruises, large patches of black and blue, scratches to his face, his hands and fingers disjointed and at odd angles, and then two large burgundy red slashes across his stomach, looking like large eyes in a Cubist painting. She tried to step away from Harry, but she was suppressed, restrained as if by some invisible manacles. He reached out to her. She screamed like a terrified child. She wanted to run, but couldn't. Harry hugged her. Her breathing sharpened as if she had been drenched in ice-cold water. Her chest tightened, her body winded from the shock. But she could not stop Harry enveloping his arms around her. He whispered her name in her ear and she felt her core melt like wax. She recognised his voice and in it a million wonderful and sad memories swirled around her like kaleidoscopic butterflies. She felt as if she would collapse, but Harry held her up and whispered his final hours to her:

'I would never have left you sitting in the café on your own, never been late for you. That was the night I wanted to tell you everything. How I really felt about you. How much

I loved you. I still do. I wanted you. I wanted us to be together, to create an exciting life together. I had saved up for us to travel when we finished our exams and wanted us to move in together. Aurora, you were my world. The only person to really understand me.

'I was just about to leave home to meet you when my father started arguing with my mother again. He started beating her almost immediately. She had no chance if I didn't intervene. I called the police and then pulled him away. My mother was bleeding, crouching in the corner of the kitchen. As I went to her, he grabbed me, pulled me back and fell on top of me, punching me and bashing my head on the ground. But all I could think of was you, that I would be late to see you, so I just pushed and kicked him off me. It was the first time I had been strong enough and brave enough to do that. The look in his eyes was pure hatred. He knew he had lost. I turned to take my mother out of the house, to take her to the neighbours so that I could at least call you. I heard one of the kitchen drawers open, turned back and saw him come at me with a knife. I stood up to face him, but he was too close and stabbed me twice—here. I fell on my knees and he knocked me unconscious. He put an end to my life and I couldn't get to you. My last thoughts were of you and my mother.

'You know I would never have left you. I want you to know that so you can release me from the box you've put me in. Let go of me now, Aurora. Let go.'

Aurora woke up crying. It was still dark. She climbed out of bed and opened the window. Gasping for fresh cool air she realised she would have to deal with the other two men in her life, whether or not she wanted to. Her tears, now etched on her face, had stopped as she remembered the detailed horror of Harry's final night, the night they were supposed to meet. All those repressed details, ignored emotions and forgotten pain. Harry's rising in her consciousness determined her next actions in this life.

*

Oliver and Aurora had kept in touch by messaging one another. Neither of them wanted to talk to each other about what had happened and what was happening between them. If it was spoken out loud, it was real. But after Aurora's nightmare and what she believed was Harry's ghost, as ridiculous as it was, she knew she would have to be the one to make the difficult decisions to move things forward. Aurora knew exactly what outcome she wanted with David and she felt that now, luckily, she would finally get that. But with Oliver, she was unsure. Unsure because she knew she still wanted him. But would she be willing to make all the compromises? To her it seemed as if that was what Oliver was expecting. He was so used to having his own way and people doing what he wanted, he could no longer be the one compromising. And that worried her. She couldn't live another life with a person who would dominate her in this way. She had worked hard, emotionally and physically, to create the life she had. And that was what made it hard for her. How far was she willing to go for this relationship? How far could she push Oliver to commit? After this last episode, he seemed to compartmentalise his emotions and needs, but this wasn't how she dealt with things.

All of her past traumas were escaping into the open. Like Pandora's box, she had released the evils in her life, but she didn't want to believe that Oliver was a part of that. She didn't think she knew him well enough and yet...

There were signs. Should she ignore them, make excuses for him as she had done with David? Or should she expose him, show him what he was really like to himself? Would he be able to handle that kind of introspection and psychoanalysis? Would she be able to cope with the potential fallout that would bring? And how would Oliver react towards her if she exposed him to himself?

She was struggling with this. She knew Jennie would support any decision she made, and Mike was ready to step in to tell Oliver 'what he needed to hear'. Ultimately, Aurora knew she was the one who had to talk to Oliver, in person, not hide behind phone messages and pretend work discussions. She asked Jennie to take a walk with her and they found their way to Golders Hill Park.

'I'm scared, Jennie.'

'Of what, which part of all of this?' asked Jennie.

'You're forcing me to be explicit, and I know that is what I need to do, but to think something and then say it out loud is very different. I'm scared of losing Oliver. I know

I hardly know him, but he's suddenly closed off from me and he seems cold at the moment. I think that is just his way of reacting. He's waiting for me to come to him. That's what he's used to. But, my God, what if he rejects me completely?' said Aurora shivering.

She looked even paler to Jennie now.

'Aurora, I am here for you and I will support any decision you make. I can't and won't tell you what to do because you will work it out yourself. You always do. I think you are one of those people who deep down inside knows everything about yourself and those around you. You have that innate human knowledge. You just ignore it sometimes.'

Aurora looked at Jennie. This was the second time she had underestimated her friend.

'Thank you, Jennie,' she said, hugging her. The tears ran down her cheeks; guilt, pride, love and regret all escaped.

They walked back to Jennie's and Aurora packed her bags to go home. It had been five days since David's attempted kidnapping, but it felt like Aurora was entering another person's life. She took a taxi to give her some time to herself, time to adjust, time to find her instinct and work out her strategy.

*

By the time she reached the apartment building, her perspective had changed. She didn't recognise it as familiar; it was now a strange new building. She entered the lobby and stairwell. Images of the chase flashed before her as she looked up again only to see a pattern of stairs and bannisters. She took her first step up. The rest came easily until she reached her front door. Her autopilot had kicked in, otherwise she wouldn't have remembered her flat number. The door still looked the same. Nothing had changed, but what was waiting for Aurora beyond the door?

She unlocked the door and stood staring into what was her flat, as if waiting for an invitation to enter. She shook herself out of this stupor. This was ridiculous, this feeling of being disjointed and separate from what had been her place of independence, her space. But as soon she had walked into the flat, she was absorbed into a confluence of David and her past self. She stood still, letting her mind run through the images and emotions, as if she were watching a film of her own life. The scenes forced feelings of nausea, insecurity, fear, power, rage and acceptance to wash through her over and over again. She was rolling through the event, and each time its impact was a little less, a little fainter, as if it was a watercolour being washed out.

She'd been standing in her flat for nearly an hour when her phone rang. She felt she was running through the last few cycles of her emotions and ignored the phone call. She had to complete this process. She felt ready to walk through her flat, reclaim her space and take back what David had tried to take away from her. It wasn't the physical aspect but the psychological takeover of her space that was important. It was her space again.

She showered, put on the washing machine and tidied up. Clean bedding, clean towels, some hoovering and it was a new flat. Her phone rang, she had forgotten to check if there were any messages. It was the police with an update. David had been released on bail until a court date was set for the hearing. They hoped it would be only a few more days, considering the seriousness of the charge. He confirmed the bail conditions were such that he was to stay away from Aurora's town completely. The offer of a victim support officer was made again, but Aurora declined and thanked them for what they were doing. She appreciated the acknowledgement of David's crime, the acknowledgement of his personality (they hadn't believed his false account) and their offer of support. She was unsure why he was allowed bail, but at least there were conditions. David wouldn't risk more than he was already losing. She thanked them again. The detective asked her if she was OK. Was she sure? Was she really OK? Aurora felt a deep pull in her chest. Yes, she was more than OK because she knew there were people looking out for her. She thanked him again, a personal thank you for his personal touch. After the call, she thought about David, out there somewhere, still free, still able to live his life while he had wanted to control hers. Was she scared? Not anymore, not of him.

But now she would have to make the phone call that terrified her more than anything else. She didn't feel ready for this now. But there was no way of putting it off any longer. Oliver had hardly kept in touch with her while she was at Jennie's. She looked at her phone and felt her insides drop out of her as if she had been pushed out of a plane at high altitude. Taking a deep breath, she pulled his number up and threw the phone away. Not now, not like this. She needed to find herself first. She had to be the Aurora that could manage Oliver, the ideal Aurora he had fallen in love with.

*

Aurora woke up after a fitful night's sleep, or 'un-sleep' as she experienced it. She couldn't shake the wretchedness from her mind. Her ground was shifting again and this time it felt like an earthquake: uncontrollable trembling where she couldn't force her ground back into place. She needed some routine to find some solidity in her life. To return to work and the recognisable every day.

Her phone oscillated between pings and screams. What had been going on? This was not a few days' worth of her usual notifications. She started to read the content.

She fell onto the sofa as the reality of what had been happening in the wider world, in *her* wider world, gradually, drop by drop, seeped into her subconscious. The messages, the articles, the photographs, the gossip, the lies, the fantasies and the reality of fame were cascading like an unstoppable waterfall, exposing Aurora as a victim of her ex-husband's kidnap attempt and her relationship with Oliver. There was even a suggestion that Oliver had arranged the kidnapping. Interspersed in the negative articles were the Morpheme tour dates. When had that been published? The band and the management seemed to be keeping quiet: no quotes or statements about anything other than the tour.

Whatever emotional stock Aurora had left was washed away by the torrent of exposure. Oliver would never forgive her now. She had lost everything. The thin line between anonymity and fame had been crossed. The life she had so painfully rebuilt was completely destroyed. Both David and Oliver were to take responsibility for this. One for his actions, the other for his response. She understood now why Oliver had kept his distance from her. He no longer wanted her in his life. It was over. But she had to hear this from him. She didn't want to be filling in the emotional gaps he was leaving in her life. She had to call him. Taking a deep breath, she tapped her mobile.

*

'Hi.'

'Hello.'

'I thought I would give you some space and time to deal with the incident. How are you?'

'Where can I start? I don't even know what I feel anymore, let alone how I am. I only know that despite everything that has happened recently, I miss you and hope you still want to work with me at least.'

'I'm sorry you feel that way. I didn't leave you alone because I didn't want us to be together anymore. That wasn't my intention. I just feel I can't give you the support you need to deal with the David issue.'

'Oh. Is that why you didn't call me when I was at Jennie's?'

'Yeah. Look, I'm not any good at the conflict resolution kind of thing, especially if it doesn't involve me directly, but I do really care about you. I want you in my life.'

'You *care* about me? So you no longer love me?'

'I don't think we should have this conversation over the phone. Where are you now?'

'I'm back at home. David has been dealt with by the police. I'm waiting to hear about a court date. So, I guess it's safe.'

'Are there no paparazzi there?'

'No. They probably saw there wasn't anyone at home. Thank God my parents are abroad!'

'You know it was David that leaked that stuff to the media?'

'Yes, I realised that when he was here talking to me.'

'The taxi driver sold his story about the David incident and it didn't take long for people to make the connections. The crazy thing about all of this is that it's done wonders for our ticket sales, Chris and Robin are thrilled with the publicity. Suddenly, Morpheme are back on the music scene. Huh, as if we ever left!'

'So the tour is still going ahead then?'

'Yeah.'

'But you don't need me there anymore?'

'It's up to you.'

'It's not up to *me*. *You* wanted me. *You* wanted me on this tour, but you're not saying that now.'

'No. Aurora, I'm a bit messed up. I'm sorry. You were everything that I wanted, but after this episode, I don't know, it feels like I'm exposed to all sorts of risks with you. I feel you're a completely different person to the you I met at the gallery. I'm not explaining myself very well.'

'No, you're not. I didn't know David was going to do this. I've been divorced from him for over two years and besides the issue with the money and a few small incidents, there wasn't anything he did to make me think he would go this far. You can't hold me responsible for his actions. Please?'

'I know. It's just how I feel right now. I'm sorry. Aurora? Look, I'll talk to Chris, we can still get you some interviews with the band. And there isn't anyone else I would rather write about us than you. I'll ask Chris to call you.'

'If that's all you want from me, forget it. I don't want your pity. That wasn't what our relationship meant to me.'

'Fine. I'm sorry I fucked up again. I think we need to end this conversation. I'm sorry. Bye.'

'I'm sure you are.'

*

Aurora was too exhausted to cry. She fell into a dead sleep as if she would never wake up again.

Slowly, Aurora came back into being and nothingness as the conversation with Oliver revisited her.

She had to find the 'normal' again, whatever that looked like. Move on. She wanted to stay in bed, be kind to herself and not have to tolerate any more abuses, but she knew she had to get up, had to push, had to claim back her working life and career at least something from this mess.

After a hot shower, a strong tea and a toasted bagel, she felt she could tackle the work at least. Her desk was still a mess from the incident with David. She was angry to the point where everything had to be moved, cleaned and then put back in order before she could start on the work itself. Logging on, she caught up with emails and projects. Evidently, not everyone had seen the stories about her and Oliver as she had so many requests for her time. She didn't know how she was going to fit it all in. And then an email from Rachel. How had she missed this on her phone?

'How are you, Aurora? If you need to talk, call me. We still want to work with you.'

It shot through her. The openness, the support, the real care from people she hardly knew.

She called Rachel and left a message. It was enough. They understood each other. Then she went back to her work. Lost in all the activities, she could forget some of the pain and distress which had been keeping her company. By the end of the day, she had ten interviews and six invitations to music nights over the next fortnight. Everyone she spoke to was too polite to mention the mess so she ignored it too.

Each day without Oliver was harder as work plunged her back into his world of music and performance. Everywhere she posted articles and read reviews, Morpheme were there. Photos of the band circulated in all the usual music magazines and social media streams. Reading through the articles, she found they were lacking, there was no real insight into the new material or the dynamics of Morpheme. Words flew through her mind and before she had even acknowledged what she was doing, she was writing the article that should have been written.

Posting it on her blog as an essay-cum-opinion piece, Aurora wondered if it would get any attention, given the volume of online content currently on the band. But she didn't care. Writing the article had been cathartic. She reclaimed a little bit of herself and smiled as she closed her laptop for the day.

*

Aurora walked to the Café Ambrose. The previous fortnight had been a whirlwind of meetings, interviews and music evenings, lots of people and writing. Emotionally, she almost felt like herself. And she finally felt excited about something. She was meeting Rachel and John to discuss some work and when they could catch up on tour.

She entered the café, scanning the tables and chairs and saw Rachel and John sitting in the corner sofa. They had found the best seat. She smiled and waved as she walked towards them.

'Hi Aurora. It's so good to see you,' said Rachel standing up to hug Aurora.

John waited his turn patiently, smiling.

'Hi Aurora. How are you?' he asked holding her hand.

'I'm fine. You know, getting there,' she smiled weakly. Why had that question affected her so? John squeezed her hand before letting her sit down.

They ordered mocktails and mezze.

'How have you been? We were really shocked when we saw the articles about your ex. What's happened with that? You don't have to say if you don't want to, but we were really concerned about you and we couldn't get through to you,' said Rachel.

'Really, I am fine. To be honest, that wasn't the biggest issue I had to deal with. I know that sounds ridiculous given that David would have done something violent, but it was the fallout with Oliver that has caused me more problems. But I've moved on from that now. I can see you don't believe me, really,' laughed Aurora feeling like a child with protective parents.

The food and drinks arrived and they tucked in.

'Well, we have some good news. Not only have we now extended our recording contract with the record company, but, well, Rachel, you tell Aurora...'

'Terry and I are engaged,' smiled Rachel.

Aurora was overwhelmed with joy.

'Congratulations! I wish you all the best, but you know the two of you are made for each other. You are those people who stay together forever. You are very lucky and I am so thrilled for you both,' said Aurora reaching over to give Rachel a hug.

'We would love it if you could come to our engagement-stroke-recording-contract party. It's only going to be a small affair with our family and friends, and we class you in that group, Aurora. Please come.'

'Of course, I'll come. Send me the details. I feel privileged. No, I really do. You don't know how happy you've made me,' Aurora replied, wiping her mouth with the napkin to regain her composure.

'We would also like to work with you to promote our new album. When we mentioned your name to the music management, they were really impressed we knew you. In fact, I think our interview with you and our claim to knowing you influenced how much we got out of the contract. Aurora, we are the lucky ones. You saw something in us, which others didn't see then and that's why we are here now. I know we would have made it, but we made it a lot sooner with you,' said John.

'You really know how to make me feel good. Thank you, I really appreciate you saying that,' replied Aurora smiling.

'Have you seen this article? It was only published a couple of days ago, but it solidifies your position as the top music journalist in the industry. It even questions whether it is your influence that has saved Oliver's career and put Morpheme back on the music map,' said Rachel passing her phone to Aurora.

Aurora took the phone. The words on the screen swam in and out of each other, taking a few seconds to settle down. That was when she saw her name, Oliver's name, and her work analysed. It was the first time she had read anyone else's analysis of her work. It was in-depth and flattering. All was good until she reached the final paragraphs analysing her ability to bring success to new bands and long-gone musicians. Oliver and Morpheme were noted as benefitting from their close relationship with someone of 'such calibre'. Aurora's stomach deflated like a balloon, replacing it with nausea. She felt cold, as if her core had just been extinguished. How many more shocks could she cope with? When she finished reading, she just looked up and stared at the wall behind Rachel.

Rachel and John looked at each other.

'Are you OK, Aurora?' asked Rachel leaning in.

'Yes, fine. Will you excuse me for a minute?' she lied, handing back Rachel's phone and rushing to the toilet.

The evacuation was inevitable. She was now confident she had lost Oliver. Her dream had evolved into the nightmare. What should have been the highlight of her career so far was the destruction of her perfect relationship. How could she navigate between the personal and business, the private and public? Her whole life of work and play had smeared into one big off-grey mess, like a polluted river. Aurora rinsed her mouth out several times, but the foulness lingered. She did her best to normalise her appearance. Would Rachel and John see beyond Aurora's face? She returned to the table and ordered a lemonade.

'Can we look at some meeting times? The management want to meet you too and also want to discuss terms as we said we would only work with *you* on articles and books,' said John.

'Yes. I really want to work with you and I think my dates will be a lot more flexible now. So yes, let's discuss the detail in a meeting. I should have my dates settled by then,' Aurora replied, her voice cracking. She took another sip of her drink.

Rachel sent Aurora the party invitation.

'I'm looking forward to seeing Terry and Brandon again. It seems like such a long time since I've seen them,' said Aurora searching for a way out of the discomfort she felt.

Aurora finished off the glass of lemonade, but she would need something a lot stronger to combat the decaying taste that lingered.

They left the café and Rachel hugged Aurora tight.

'Call me if you need anything,' she whispered.

'Thank you, Rachel. I will,' promised Aurora.

'Bye, Aurora. If there is anything, workwise or otherwise, just call us. You have our numbers,' said John, and there was the warm, sincere squeeze of his hand again. Just a gesture, but the meaning filled her world. Aurora rushed home and worked until she fell asleep at her desk exhausted.

*

'We need to meet,' said Oliver directly.

Aurora's mouth dried and she felt as if her heart had stopped. She had woken up on the sofa to her phone ringing. She felt like a dried-out husk.

'Where?' she whispered.

'Your place. I've got people outside my place. I'll get out the back. I'll be there in an hour.'

An hour? thought Aurora. What would her life look like in an hour?

She went into the bathroom and threw up what wasn't there. Her throat raw, her eyes sore from crying, she was a wreck. She gargled some mouthwash. It burnt through her mouth and throat. She held onto the feeling, the raw pain; it couldn't be any worse than what was coming. An hour of agony before her life was confirmed as dead. She drank a bottle of water too quickly, feeling nauseous again, but held it back. She quickly showered. Pacing the front room did nothing to rid her of the nervous energy that stung her body constantly.

Her intercom buzzed. She didn't even jump, but walked slowly over to let Oliver in, to let in the devastation that she knew was coming.

Oliver walked into the flat, closing the door behind him, gently, quietly as if he didn't want anyone to know he was there. Aurora was waiting for him in the front room. She looked awful. Had he done that to her? How? When? He didn't understand what had happened between them. But he couldn't risk what was left of his career. It wasn't working. He knew he should have kept clear, kept away from relationships. But Aurora was different, she had made him happy, she had made him think in ways he hadn't felt in years. And yet it wasn't enough for him. He was forgetting his music, his lifeline, his being. He wasn't himself anymore and it terrified him. He had every intention of cutting off the problem, but now more than ever he needed her, needed her fame, her reputation, her ideality.

'What did you want to say that you couldn't say on the phone?' demanded Aurora angrily, her voice trembling as she finished the question.

'I think we need to end this relationship.'

Aurora smiled wryly. It was just what she had expected. Now that she was standing in front of Oliver, her anger with him grew. He was saying he wanted to end it, but she felt him holding back. There was something else.

'Why? Give me a valid explanation,' demanded Aurora. She would make him work for this.

'I just think this isn't working for us on a personal level. The episode with David and now all of these articles... I kind of feel you have taken over my life, complicating everything. You know, I was fine before we met and now suddenly I'm out there again, only it's not about the music or the band, it's about my relationship with you. I want the ideality back.

I didn't realise the control it gave me over my career. This reality is not what I want. I'm sorry,' said Oliver, one minute passionate, then the next sheepishly looking at the floor.

'And I don't get a say in this at all? You are just erasing me from your life, is that it? And I'm supposed to accept it, just like I accepted your invitation to tour with you, your invitation to be a part of your life?' shouted Aurora angrily. As she lifted her head, she saw Oliver's jaw lock and his dark blue eyes squint in anger. How far could she push him? After everything he had said to her, done to her, made her fall in love and now this.

'You really can't see it in yourself, can you?' she asked.

'What?' He was hurt and she knew it.

'How you use people.'

'That's unfair,' Oliver defended himself weakly.

'No, it's not. Thinking about everything we've been through, it has been about you, the impact on you. If you see it as a positive impact, you revel in it. If you believe it is detrimental to your world-view, you want to dispose of it, cut it away, exorcise it. So that's what you're doing with me now. Something else has happened to tip the balance against me, hasn't it? Damn it, answer me!' shouted Aurora.

Oliver was shocked into a quick response. He wasn't used to people arguing back with him in this way. What did she know? *How* did she know?

'Yes, the article about you.' He looked down. He had been determined not to tell her the truth, not to show his weakness.

Aurora's body froze while her mind raced at lightning speed through the article Rachel had shown her.

'Oh my God. You're jealous!' exclaimed Aurora.

Oliver looked up at Aurora.

'Don't be ridiculous. Why would I be jealous?'

'No, but you are, aren't you? That bit about your recent success being based on knowing me. That's what this is about! You've lost your relevance.'

'My music has always had relevance. That idiot doesn't know what he's writing about.'

'Excuse me? So, you think his analysis of my work is rubbish? Is that it?'

'That's not what I said. Don't twist my words like that.'

'Well, how do you want me to twist them, because so far you've done your own twisting of our relationship into something it's not.'

'When did you start to feel so negative about me? When we first met, you were so nervous and in awe of me. I could see the love and passion in your eyes. You would do anything for me. And now you just keep questioning me. Is the reality too much for you? Is that it? What you really want is my persona, the Oliver on stage. You want to go back to the fan–artist ideality, your fantasy, don't you?'

'Firstly, you talk about me wanting the on-stage Oliver, but that is crap. It's your ego putting that into your head. Secondly, and this is what you can't see, you are nothing without your fans. How do you recognise your talent without the reflection of that talent by your fans? What you create means nothing unless others recognise it. The creative work's value is not in itself, but in what its existence means to others. If you created music just for yourself, didn't publish it, didn't promote it, just kept it to yourself, its only value would be to you. But that's not enough for you, you need the validation of others. And all the better if that attention comes from like-minded people—those connections you so like to deride. That was why you were so excited and thrilled to be recognised that night in the pub. I could see it in you that night. You crave that attention and validation. And now that has been compromised because it's no longer validation on your own merits, it's because of your association with me. This is only one article. Why are you willing to throw away so much based on so few words by someone you don't even know?'

'It's not just a few words. Everyone will see that. You are right, it questions my legitimacy as an artist. Everything I've worked for and towards, has now been swept away by one article and YOU are the constant reminder of that. Don't you see how impossible it is for me to stay with you?'

'We were lucky to find each other. There *is* a strong connection between us. Look at everything we've been through. Despite that, you're here in person talking to me. Admit it, you're scared. ADMIT IT!' shouted Aurora, tears filling her eyes.

Oliver was bending over the top of the sofa as if Aurora had punched him, winding him completely. And he thought *he* would be the one doing all the wounding. He recognised the fear she identified so surgically.

'I can't be the man you want me to be. I don't *want* to be the man you want me to be. And yes, that does scare me. You know why? Because I feel I'm losing control over my life. I don't know any other life outside of music. If I don't have that, I have nothing. And yes, you may be right about the ego. But I wouldn't expect you to understand that as you've had people telling you what to do most of your life.'

Aurora felt the sentence skewer her like an arrow. How could any reconciliation come out of this war of words?

She closed her eyes and took a deep breath. Why would he never entertain anyone else's feelings or concerns as legitimate?

'You've just done what you say you hate fans doing to you. You've projected your shallow experience of your life onto me. You think you know me so well that you can make that comment. Well you know, projection works both ways. You assume an awful lot of other people and you never give them any allowances. You expect me to be the supportive I-forgive-you-anything fan. I should be grateful for your attention and your time. But I'm not that person,' whispered Aurora. The fight had drained her spunk. Then she added, 'Why did you come here, really?'

'I need you to do this tour with me,' said Oliver quietly, but clearly.

'Arrgh,' sighed Aurora, who'd run out of tears.

'You can arrange everything with Chris and Robin,' said Oliver, his voice jarring with emotion. Aurora looked up at him. His jaw was working in that way when he was angry, and yet... Aurora looked into his eyes, those beautiful blue eyes, those eyes that were still young and passionate, those eyes that were now crying.

Despite every nerve in her body screaming at her not to dive in further, she walked over to Oliver. She stood by him, behind the sofa, only a foot away, with a chasm of infinite depth to step over. Her final move would pitch her into the abyss. She reached out her hand, feeling static all around her, stinging her body as her arm extended closer. Oliver didn't move. His head bent down as tears fell unabated. His hands were gripping the top of the sofa. Aurora's hand felt for his, her soft skin calmed the fist into submission.

For a couple of seconds they stayed like that, unsure of the next move that would decide their futures. Aurora stood, holding, gripping, almost ready to let go if she had to. But this would be her last chance after all the pain they had inflicted on each other. It was a testing battle, pushing the one you cared about away, shoving, hurting, taking aim and firing, all to see if they were 'the one', the person that would love you beyond life.

In the next instant, Oliver made the decision for them. He grabbed Aurora by the arms, pushing her back towards the wall, he looked straight into her eyes, his tears still flowing, his eyes questioning her face. Like a maniac, unsure of where to start, he searched for what he needed, could see, could feel in her tightening grip of him, that she would never give him up. He would always have his reflection.

Aurora pulled him towards her, even while she was rammed up against the wall. She had never felt such an intense passion and all she wanted at that moment was to fall with Oliver into a never-ending abyss, together, away from the world, just the two of them locked together. Oliver's mouth brushed her cheek, his eyes closed as if in pain, his mouth seeking every millimetre of her every pore, every cell that made her being. He found her mouth and they fell into each other. His hands embraced every part of her body, from her face and neck to her back and waist, her buttocks, held tight, pulling her leg up and seeking her inside. All he wanted to do was make her his.

She was right, he needed her more than she needed him. It wasn't until he realised what losing her from his life really meant that he had given up his proud fight. He had lost the battle and the war, only to find Aurora giving him his freedom. He couldn't live without her; he was certain of that now. He wanted to feel her body, hear her heart, breathe her breath.

Aurora held onto Oliver, almost hugging the life out of him as he caressed and kissed her with an urgency she had never felt in her life. She felt him all over her, his body duplicating hers in every tremble, every kiss, every gasp of air. She didn't want to think anymore. She was exhausted from the loss and fright she had had. Her body and mind ached as if she'd been battered in a storm. She only wanted to complete the fall into the darkness, holding onto Oliver and never letting go. They kissed ferociously, seeking all their wants in each other, finally opening up entirely and exposing what they had fought to keep safe and hidden from each other. They fell to the floor, no longer able to support each other. They sought each other inside clothes, removing all obstacles to their intimacy. Aurora felt as if her chest would burst with the emotion she felt. She could not name it. This emotion went beyond love; it filled the universe and her mind as she felt Oliver inside her. They moved together, moved through space and time, but always together, now fashioned together for life.

The End...

Aurora and Oliver sat in a wood-panelled room. They were waiting to be called into the magistrate's court. It had been a long wait already. There was activity outside the door every now and then and they anticipated being called, but then the activity died down.

The room had been full of people when they had arrived, but slowly the crowd had thinned to just the two of them.

'How do you feel?' asked Oliver for the fifth time.

'Tired, but OK. This needs to be done,' replied Aurora having given different answers every time. She smiled through the tiredness. 'How about you?'

'Nervous. Like you said, it has to be done. I just don't want to let you down,' he replied smiling weakly.

He brought her hand up to his face and kissed her palm. Aurora closed her eyes, feeling the full warmth of his breath seep through her hand, arm, shoulder and chest. All she wanted to do was melt into his arms.

The door opened and the investigating detective and prosecutor walked in. They both looked despondent and tired. Aurora shivered. Oliver stood up ready to go.

'I'm afraid we have some news.'

'There's been an accident. David won't be attending court.'

Aurora looked down. Visions of a mangled motorbike surfaced.

'What's happened? Is he in hospital?' asked Oliver, panicking and thinking through a hundred different scenarios.

They sat down next to Aurora. She stared at them as Oliver put his arm around her.

'I'm afraid David died in the accident. We haven't got all the details yet, but it appears he jumped in front of an oncoming train. He left a bag on the platform, providing us with information about the court case and keys to his house. There is clear evidence of his activities stalking you. I'm really sorry.'

David was dead. He could no longer harm her. He would no longer be a threat to her, her parents or Oliver. She sucked in her breath, put her head in her hands and cried. She cried but was out of tears, her body wracked with relief that she was finally free of him.

'What happens now?' asked Oliver.

'Well, nothing. The case is dismissed. My condolences. I know we were here today for a reason, but I presume there was a time you had a good relationship with him?'

Aurora looked up. Why was it that when someone died, people were sorry, even when that person was evil. Why?

'Thank you, but you don't need to console me. I'm relieved he's dead. You cannot understand the weight that I was carrying around because of him. And now it's gone. I feel free.'

Aurora turned to Oliver.

'We can get on with our lives now,' she said hugging him tightly.

*

Aurora could feel the push and pull of the crowd around her. There was a buzz, an excitement rippling through the space. She was encased in human beings. She felt strange and familiar at the same time. Past experiences and dreams had merged into one where she couldn't separate reality from dreamscape. Then it all went black and the crowd was hushed into silence. A blue light pulsed from the back of the stage and a mist appeared, defining the boundaries of the blue light. The pulsating increased its area on stage. There was a hushed anticipation as Aurora watched and waited.

A crash of drums and base tore through the space, ripping up the silence and granting the crowd permission to scream. She felt the thrust and power of the crowd's energy as they jumped and screamed to the beat of the music.

Oliver appeared on stage, the crowd screaming even louder until the sound smothered the space. Morpheme performed their biggest hit song, causing the crowd to convulse like an earthquake.

The blue lights drowned the stage, making Morpheme look ethereal, inhuman. As the song came to an end, Oliver was preparing for his biggest note, pushing all his passion through it, nailing it completely. As the song ended, the lights softened to a creamy moonlight, spotlighting Matt, Craig, Nathan, Nick and Oliver. The crowd roared their approval.

Oliver scanned the audience, and finding the face he recognised, he smiled and winked at Aurora. For her, ideality and reality became one.

THE END

hands

9 781803 816500

Mazey Ways

Nan Rudden

Mazey Ways

PALORES PUBLICATIONS' 21st CENTURY WRITERS

Nan Rudden
Mazey Ways

May 2007

ISBN   0-9551878-7-7
          978-0-9551878-7-2

Designed and printed by:

ImageSet,
63 Tehidy Road,
Camborne,
Cornwall.
TR14 8LJ
01209 712864

Published by:

Palores Publications,
11a Penryn Street,
Redruth,
Cornwall.
TR15 2SP

Dedicated
to my family

grateful thanks to
Joy Batten for the cover photo.

Contents

SEA-SIDE

"Oh, what a big water," says the child,
Spreading his arms to indicate immensity.
The sands stretch out in static dunes.
It is the sea where undulations are alive,
Each rippling line unique,
Sighing and sucking as it falls and ebbs.
Here the tide is tame, smooth sand and shallow sea,
A mild blue playground, summer safe.
"Why can't we stay for ever?" asks the child.
Old women smile, then sigh,
Thinking of those who did indeed remain
On and in and under that same sea;
Sea-green the graves that should have been grass-green.

REFLECTIONS

A woman walks towards me.
Familiar? No, not quite.
Figure gross, face more grim
Than I remember. Why! The wall's
A mirror. It is myself I see
Grown old, obese, waddling across the room.
Ah well, I never made the most of
Any looks I had, and now
It seems I've lost them anyway.
So smile, you sourpuss image,
Speech, sparkle if you get the chance,
Impress with usefulness.
And none may notice, as now I do,
The girl's become a gargoyle.

STARDUST

She was so beautiful, so beautiful,
Looking for love this time, so we were told
By those who knew the secrets of the stars,
The lives spread out across the centrefold.
I saw her once, the day that she came here
To open that big store which now has closed.
So ladylike, you never would have thought
She was the model girl who once had posed
On calendars. But she was unknown then,
Before her face fixed on our inner eye,
The lips so red, the hair like polished brass.
And still we ask, why did she have to die?
She smiled at me, and so she's smiled at you.
Through knowing me, you are immortal too.

LICENCED TO KILL

With one hand I grasp the legs and wingtips
And with the other
I grip the feathered neck in a knuckled vice.
The bird merely gives a blink.
Used to being handled, how could it know its fate?
Don't worry, these birdbrains cannot think.

But as I don't want to bother
The rest of the batch, I turn from the crate.
With little finger beneath the beak, I lift the head
To right angles. The strength is in the wrist.
Control the downward pull, no violent heave,
No sudden jerk to take the head right off and leave
The arterial hosepipe to spout and twist.

In spasms life discharges in my hold
While the blood drains neatly into the internal gap.
Last twitch. Now I am able
To pass the carcase, slap
It down on the pluckers' bench, next phase to
Poulterers' slab and dinner table.
I kill to eat.
My part in the primeval lineage.
Also I kill to meet
The problem of compassion
When suffering becomes insufferable pain.
The farmer keeps the powers
Society feels unable to retain.

Yet not far off in time or place or memory
The ceremonial feast incorporated
The aged wise chief, or virile enemy.
Then the tender, young, raw cabin boy
Ranked less than officers and crew.

Mazey Ways

Who was it said we should not unduly strive
To keep alive the ailing? Of course we knew
That breaking necks was the right ploy
To free society from crime.

With the devaluation of the soul
We superior animals count our time
Solely in this world, and so our bodies must endure
Beyond reason, parts more precious than the whole.
Pneumonia's no more the old man's friend
Quickening the last illness to a speedy end.

Were I politically correct I might feel bound
To fence a penal colony for fighting cocks and found
A hospice for the weakly chicks.

Last one. All done. My pluckers chat.
Ankle-deep in lousy feathers, they mix
Jokes and gossip, while guts drop
Into buckets from the trussing table.
Plumped white breasts. Bloody slop.
But this is a domestic scene. Bear in mind
Its no vast abattoir, no killing field
Where tented surgeons chat and joke
To blunt the horror as they wield
Their knives to eviscerate and truss their own kind.

Should we all eat grain?
John Barleycorn must die.
The breaking of bread relies on
Breaking the bonds in rain
And air and earth by the powered Sky-
Force taken from the slowly dying sun.
Take. Eat. Develop. Die.
Take a turn as dust, until
The wheel of life recycles by.
Meanwhile my little flock will feed us.

Gwlasow

I walked again last night in the country of my dreams.
Amnesiac months, a year can pass,
But every time when I return
Nothing has changed. Even the weather is the same.
I see the everlasting hills,
Tread the footpaths' springing turf,
Look down on slate-grey roofs
And swoop into the narrow lanes,
Floating past terraced, granite cottages
To the harbour and the boats.
"Take me out," I cry, but the crew
Always say that it's too rough beyond the bar.
Don't they know that I can sail? That years ago
My parents took me on an ocean ship
To the land that's never seemed like home?
But they're right. I want to stay.
I know the place so well although
I've never seen it with my waking eyes.

Time for the duty call on my old aunt. I go
The long way round, for I shan't find her house
In its maze of Cornish streets unless I reach the fork
From where that little lane will lead me.

This time I'm here. We sit and talk.
But what we say I never can recall.
I've not seen her, nor anyone I know,
In a tiny house like this.

Did the wall
Dissolve? I'm in the street again, flitting fast,
Trying to see more before the dream dissolves.
Can hauntings come not only from the past
But also from the future? Can it be
That aged aunt's myself, forgetful, worn,
The visitor some niece as yet unborn?
If that is true, I know this exile will return.

SIMPLE GIFT

God is Mother, states the feminist,
More merciful than the militant Father-figure.
Oh! Says the startled child
Was Jesus man or woman
Or both at once? Horrible image,
Worse than the reality of Calvary.
The crucified were not covered. There was
No loincloth on the Cross. No doubt
Until the present disbelief
Discredited decorum.
Artists make God in the image of their age,
And we attach our values.
Blessed be the child whose faith stays
Secure in the Holy Family.

VALEDICTION

The wild beast's roar
Is no more.
Adrenaline is triggered by the starter's gun.
Ever faster,
Body's master,
Heart and lungs obey until the needless race is won.
On the course
The goaded horse
Lacks the will to win that spurs the motivated man.

Soon lay down
The laurel crown,
The medallist today becomes tomorrow's also-ran.
Yield up
The silver cup,
Youngsters in a hurry count down the fractioned time.
Take a look
At record book,
Every dusty name was once a winner in his prime.
Record broken,
Athlete's token,
The muscle-bound mean something more by barrier of pain.
What now the prize?
A slow demise,
Fame faded, joints replaced, pacemaker, cripple's cane.

MAZEY WAYS

It must have been monotonous
Following hypnotic heels,
Measuring the miles
Along the ruthless roads.
The military mind
Mapped with planned precision
The horizontal plumblines
Of the rule of Rome.

Milestones and monuments stand singly;
Celtic circles cluster on the hills.
The wily ones waited
Until the single-minded went
Or were assimilated.

Now the native network overlays
The spider webs of straight streets.
Roads invite around the contour curves;
Little lanes turn to tempt the traveller.

But still in legend legionaries
March across the moors.
Phalanxes of phantoms,

                           dead

                                    straight.

ASTRONAUT

Stretch, child,
Delivered from the sheltering womb.
Stand, climb,
Excite admiration.
Raise your voice,
Lift your eyes,
Make it to the mountain top.
Snap to attention,
Poised like Stylites,
Summit of achievement,
Pinnacle of perfection.
Menhir, pillar,
Perpendicular spire,
Point to the divine.
Revere the vertical,
Escape earth's gravity.
Set your sights on the stars.

FEMALE PRINCIPLE

Ever since Eva woman takes the blame,
Needed and necessary,
Encouraged to be seductive,
Expected to be sexually submissive,
Feared if she flaunts her fecundity.

In men's imagination
Maidens are meant to be rescued,
Romanced and married,
But may become monstrous mothers.

Kali, both creator and destroyer,
Medea, Medusa, Morgan, Lady Macbeth.
Slay the bitch!
Burn the fascinating witches!

Ave, Maria, safely sexless,
Somehow maiden and mother,
Simultaneously satisfying,
Best of both worlds.
At last a fitting woman to be worshipped,
No occasion of sin,
Pure perfection,
Blameless.

SCAPEGOAT

Hey. You, stranger!
What's your name?
No reply? How rude!
How satisfying.
I'll unload the blame
For what I've done
and what I'm going to do
On you.
Legitimately point the finger.
Obviously you're not our sort,
Those rumours must be true,
We can believe that press report.
Don't go away! Just linger,
We need you in our community.
There's nothing like collective loathing
To solidify unity.
Too true,
We must defend ourselves
Against the likes of you,
Thief, adulterer, aggressor, liar.
Ours is the right to retaliate;
You were the first to fire.

MUSEUM PIECE

Twenty thousand years or so before our time,
A man fashioned from mammoth ivory
Belly, buttocks, mammaries
Of a fecund female, the so-called
Paleolithic Venus

Rows of Mother Goddesses sit comfortably
Cradling cornucopia,
Baskets of bread beside them,
Sheaf in one arm, baby in the other.

When did Venus float into
Men's minds?
Golden Princess in her ivory tower,
Willing to be won, perhaps, by wooing,
Required to prove virginity,
Slim girl, awaiting impregnation.

Can maid and mother meld?
Desire and need at last combined.
A miracle to satisfy
The imagination of mankind.

RELAY

The fear of God we have forgot.
To each their own belief is now our creed.
The Church is neither cold nor hot
But, standing by, fulfils the need
Of those who use it for the rites
Of passage, making doubly sure
That social obligation's heights
Are duly marked, and ask for nothing more.

The Greek and Roman gods became
Mere figures in a childhood story book.
The Norsemen's gods bequeathed a name
To days; their worshippers forsook
Them for a God we think so mild
That now we do not care to take a stand
Against the rational or wild.

Pan still lives, and from another land
A fervent faith is strengthening which, in turn
Will spread the holy fire to cleanse and burn.

WEDLOCK

More than friendship, more than lust,
What is this thing called love?
Mysterious pair bonding, each
Valuing the other above
The rest, at least when love is new.

Oh the sweet agonies of courtship,
Delicious yearnings of romance ,
Looks, gestures, words and gifts make up
The trappings of the ritual dance,
Ensure commitment's due.

Regenerating generations,
Parents calculate the length
Of silken thread to weave the web
Of family trees, whose tensile strength
Will keep the coupling true.

HUMAN NATURE

The press of people passes, the field is full of folk.
Each estimates the other at a glance.
Age, sex, status, acceptable or not,
Wondering if someone met by chance
Could be of use. The entity is judged
By what's expressed, the look of the external,
Without the thought that some rough husk
Might hold a sweet and perfect kernel
And balanced beauty hide a bitter core.
Where is the inner life? What is the soul?
Do we never shed our seventh veil?
The coil within each cell contains the whole
Blueprint, expresses one small part
Appropriate to the situation,
Fitting into some neat, great, master-chart.
The embryonic cell divides unchecked
Until, in time, each knows its place
And function. The wooden puppet's nose
Grows longer with each lie, distorts his face,
Or so the fairy-story goes.
Our noses grow, repair, maintain,
Stay within their destined bounds,
Remain no more, no less, retain
Their nature. Only the cancerous cell
Proliferates without the usual brakes,
Undifferentiated, wild.
Indifferent is the havoc that it makes.
What happens when we lose control?
The many deadly weapons which we wield
Make a sport called ethnic cleansing.
People pass; the folk are buried in the field.

THE WAY

How odd of God
To choose the Cross,
Symbol of loss,
Hallowed gallows,
Cruel jewel
To hang on a golden chain.

What is life but strife?
Why bother
About another?
When everyone
Strives for the sun
Why seek suffering and pain?

Paradise lost is the cost
To egocentric man.
God's planned way
Does not repay
Eye for eye,
Nails high the message on a tree.

I have borne scorn,
Know all woes.
The price of peace
Lifts love above
The self. Vendettas cease.
Remember this when Me you see.

'THANKS FOR THE MEMORY'

"Is it really that long since we met?
Seems like only yesterday.
You're looking just the same."
(I'm hoping that you'll say the same to me.)
"You haven't changed a bit", and yet
I wonder what's the state of play.
Each day must bring a little change
Though, self-absorbed, I'll never see
How much has happened in a year of days
Unless I take a look at my day-book.

I bet you've changed, gained or lost a fortune,
Found a lover, had a child, survived
An operation. However, I won't pry
About that special friend with whom you took
A holiday. I wondered, when you seemed so shy,
If your significant other had arrived
At last, but no name came on any greetings card.

If we recounted all the years between
We'd end up feeling strangers. I'd see you
As one approaching middle age;
That point I've passed, although I know it
Only when the helpful young are seen
Deferring to us seniors, yes, including me.

Forget all that. Turn back the page.
"We can pick up where we left off," you say.
Focus. Zoom. Flash. Click. The mind's eye
Telescopes the years as images recur.
"Ah, what good times we had then, what fun."
(Troubles too, once shared, and overcome). And now?
"Is that the time already? I must fly."
"Let's arrange to meet again quite soon."
"Yeah, yeah. But now I'm late. So long, I have to run."

TYMPANUM

Paradise is a passive place.
The righteous rise, conducted by the angel band
To join the ranks of prophets, saints, musicians
Around the central Throne. While on the other hand
Sinister devils snatch the damned from Michael's scales
And pitch them into Hell, provide the feast
For most ingenious demons, whose kitchen
Mangles king and harlot, pope and merchant, pimp and priest.

The medieval masons knew this world.
Kitchens and dungeons they built, as well as castle halls.
Dread images were not hard to conjure
While fashioning oubliettes within the walls.

The Majestic gaze looks neither right nor left
But stares at us, challenging our choice.
On this far shore, which side will you be on?
Live now, pay later, suffer or rejoice.

BARTLEMAS

It is believed, the guide book states,
That once there was a pagan cult
With sacred grove and spring upon this site.
Then, because the folk would gather here,
A church was built to house the relics which
Cured leprosy and headaches and snake bite.

Did they arrive by pilgrim paths,
Congregate for hopeful veneration,
Kiss the holy caskets, ease their pain,
But hedge their bets, sprinkling with spring water?

Reformers wrecked the reliquaries, stole jewels,
Smashed bones, and changed the language once again.
Next came Cromwell's men to strip the roof of lead,
Scrape and whitewash paintings from the walls.

Roused from slumber by Victorian zeal,
The neo-Gothic builders judged this church
Was insignificant. A mere chapel
In a scruffy field, it lacked appeal.

In this centennial year its mother church
Echoes with near emptiness.

The chapel's locked
Against the so-called human dregs who lie
Under the straggling trees, avoiding
That damp patch where once there might have been
A spring. The ground is nearly dry.

MUSEUM OF MODERN ART

In desperation, daemon-driven Monet
Paid his doctor's fees with paintings.
Some were displayed only to be dismissed as
Daubs, crude bright blotches of chemical colours,
Mere impressions of nature.

Only as death drew near and eyesight dimmed,
And the lilies diffused into lilac light,
Did he at last find favour.
Now in the galleries crowds gather to gaze at
The final flowering of beauty.

I roam through ever emptier rooms,
Invited to admire the glowing abstracts and
Marvel at the manipulation of art grown angular.
Decorative, provocative, disturbing,
Clever comments to note,
Not to contemplate.

Towards the exit huge canvasses are hanging,
Form abandoned, colours rendered drab.
Black and grey are slashed across a paler grey.
An arid, aimless art that dearth of craft makes casual.
Better the brilliant daubs I think, than this dread dreariness.

Then I spy the curves and colours that I crave,
Only to find a rubbish pile of rotting fruit
And decomposing rats.
My mind tells me I am being mocked, and
This deliberate deceit dares my acceptance.
Then comes doubt. Are these disintegrating images
The artists' honest picture of our age,
Forcing us to face their desperation?

AGAN ARLUDHES

Mosaic lined, the church at Nazareth
Mirrors the Madonna. Each nation honours
Mary as their own dear Mother.

Marya Kernewek, how would we picture you?
No Saxon blue-eyed blonde, for sure;
No gold-embroidered gown in which to traipse the lanes;
You'd trip in that kimono down the quay.

Proper you'd look, demurely dressed,
A saffron shawl around your long, dark hair,
White blouse, blue skirt, neat towser clean and pressed.

Our Lady, maid and mother, full of grace,
You'd not stand poised upon a pillar, but
Welcome us with sweet and kindly face.

Queen of Angels, married to a carpenter,
You do understand our little ways.
Help of Christians, you knew joys and sorrows, pain
Of exile, longing for the days
When you could make the journey home again.

You kept the culture amid alien rule;
You kept the faith in days of seeming doom;
Blessed to greet once more the Holy Ghost,
The Comforter, with Whom you comfort us.

Myghternes nef, lowena dhys;
Dhe vercy Dew ragon-ny pys.

LIFE'S ROUTINE

I wipe the breath-steamed window of the country bus.
The night is not too dark to see the standing crops.
Silent fields, except when
Ploughed, sown, watered, fed, sprayed, harvested
By men invisible within their bright machines.
The bus stops twice along the village street.
No-one waits. Goodnight. One man steps off.
Dim lights gleam in curtained rooms.
No conversation now around the leaping fire
But contemplation of the glittering screen.
No need to ask the neighbours in;
More interesting lives can be switched on
And just as easily dismissed.
A shadow stirs. Commercial break. Put the kettle on.
By day pedestrians are few.
Incarcerated in their cars they
Drive to work, school, store,
And home again.
Population 3174;
Born, raised, nurtured, bred, employed, deceased,
The human crop's mere ciphers on a censor's list.
And yet, except for lovers newly joined,
Each item is as egocentric as myself,
And just as judgmental.

DUAL DUEL

May you fare well my once true love;
I sense it's time to part,
Slough off love's skin, and now begin
To break another heart.

May you enjoy your next affair
With all its subtle thrill;
When scheming chance serves to entrance
And captivate the will.

Ambush is the waiting ploy.
I'll wait with bated breath.
Like to like, I'll watch you strike
And be in at the death.

We can't escape each other's fate;
You've taught your pupil well.
We'll both pursue a love that's new,
And then we'll fuck and tell.

When we're sated with the game,
Or find our charm has fled,
We can but feed our mutual need
With tales of love we've shed.

ARTIFICE

When the New Jerusalem comes down to earth
What will be the fate of fleas?
Will pests and parasites, like persona non grata,
In every sense become reformed?
If lions turned to eating grass, they'd defecate,
And then we'd need bot-flies and beetles
To complete the messy, balanced cycle.

No, we'll be supplied with wholesome pets,
Formed, not procreated.
No seeds, no crops, no fruit,
But vivid, everlasting flowers will bloom,
Decorated with bright butterflies.

We'll not need to bake our bread;
Manna will be provided
In international flavours.
Last week I saw it all,
At Disney World.

MORTALITY

In my youth I never thought of death
Save as something static
Or dramatic,
Never my own.

The elderly retired to bed, smiled sweetly, and
Let their last breath
Expire in peace.
A merciful release
Before becoming tokened by tasteful, tidy stone.

The murderer held more interest than the victim.
For days, weeks, months, and even years,
Capture, trial and sentence
Tickled the senses
For little while.
Accidents, disaster, famine, wars
Occurred elsewhere. Our fears
Aroused the numbers game.
Yet praise or blame,
Bravery or guile,
Make human tales, increase sales;
Just choose one name
To champion or revile.

And now...

Thank God I've
Made it through the night
Still alive.
Take each day
At a time,
The voices say.
My body cannot move,
But can you hear
My mind? I love
You. That's all
And everything
Before last call.

FERTILITY

They can.
Can what?
Can have.
Who can?
Women can.
Have what?
Babies.
Not always.
Always risky.

Men can't.
Superfluous?
No, needed.
One act.
No responsibility.
Except -
Except what?
Care
For woman
Then for child.
Caught, but
Only if willing.

From women
Comes life.
Welcomed or dreaded,
Human beings.

Our future.

ETERNITY (PERHAPS)

The sweet flesh is so desirable.
So perfectly moulded,
That we ignore its future.
Its aging, and eventual mouldering
To bare bones.

Should I become important,
Renowned or powerful,
I would choose burial.
After worms had churned,
My bones would be exhumed
And I'd be reconstructed.

In some famous museum
I'd lie, sit, stand, or be
Concentrated in a bust.
Looking young, of course,
And reasonably lovely.

But ordinary corpses are so common.
I choose to go from earth to air.
My ashes will rest in an urn
Looking tasteful on the mantelpiece
Beside a flattering photograph.

A few generations will remember me
Before my dust joins everlasting dust.

MATHEMATICS

Ena, mena, morra, mi,
Pisca, larra, moura, li
Out goes he.

Counting, calculating,
Fingers, abacus,
Computer, calculus,
Numbers fascinate,
Figurings exasperate,
Yet fixed proportions
Reassure.

Four corners in a square,
Eight corners in a cube,
Each side symmetrical,
Each angle right.
Infinitely variable
Are width, depth, height,
But proportionately
Bound.

Six particles in one proton,
Always the same.
Up, down,
Strange, charm,
Bottom, top.
When orbited by eight electrons
Oxygen's the atom's name
And with no
Deviation.

Language lives within this frame.
Dimensions evolve.
Nouns change to verbs,
Adding, discarding,
Inventive, wounding,
Amusing, ecstatic.
In subtext of poetry
Human inheritance is
Unleashed.

PARANOIA

Sometimes at my back I see a shape, a tree.
I turn. It halts. Immovable against
The rest, unless they shield its stealth
When once I turn. I may
See it later on the wood's edge
Or silhouetted on the ridge.
I dare not enter. No chance I'd have against advance
Of the darkening ring. Each tree would reach
A twiggy limb to catch and pass and hold. What then?
Counting leaves I dread. Alive, or seeming dead,
How many on one branch? How many on one tree?
I'd struggle to surface from green depths,
Or choke beneath the dry, brown mound whose rustling sound
Echoes within my head.

THE REBELLIOUS CHILD

I hate you.
Why? Because you won't
Because you don't
Listen to me.
All right, I'll run away.
Live under that hedge.
Sleep in the tree house.
Climb up there, you?
You're too old, too stupid.
I'll tell my best friend.
He'll bring me food.
Then when I come back
You'll be sorry
And treat me nice.
If you lock me in
I'll have to kill you.
Paint in father's beer.
And you, I'll stab you.
You'll fall face down upon the table
And bleed to death.
So there!

It didn't work.
Father didn't even taste the paint.
I was so cross at lunch
I grabbed a fork.
Four small, red pricks in your arm.
Fascinating.
You thought it was an accident
And talked of table manners.

So, all this afternoon,
When your horrid friend came round,
I sat and drew her nasty face.
She was not pleased.
Later my father grinned.
"Good likeness, dear," he said,
"I think that she won't call again."
He gave me a pound.

THE COCKEREL

In the misty morning
I love to hear the cockerels crowing,
Calling their hens to eat
And clucking over grains of wheat.
Fewer eggs but lower costs
And happier hens, not squashed
In battery cages, from where
No crowing splits the morning air.

On the Crucifixion morn
What rooster heralded the dawn?
Christ was denied, Peter wept.
No one understood except
The gospel writers. So
Now we all recall that crow
And Peter's fearful sorry fall,
So much like us. God save us all.